THE CARPENTER'S APPRENTICE

Other books in this series
The Book and the Phoenix
Hostage of the Sea

STORIES OF THE SIX WORLDS

The Carpenter's Apprentice

CHERITH BALDRY

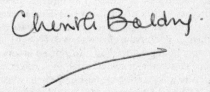

Front cover design by Vic Mitchell

ISBN 0 86065 886 4

Phoenix is an imprint of Kingsway Publications Ltd,
Lottbridge Drove, Eastbourne, E Sussex BN23 6NT.
Typeset by Nuprint Ltd, Harpenden, Herts.
Printed in Great Britain by Richard Clay Ltd, Bungay, Suffolk.

To Peter

The Pronunciation of Some Names on Fern

Cador   Cad'or ('a' as in 'cat')
Gildas   Gil'das (the 'G' is hard)
Hilarion   Hilar'ion (second syllable pronounced 'are')
Isolda   Isol'da ('i' as in 'fit')
Kynan   Ky'nan (first syllable rhymes with 'eye')
Owain   Owen
Pelidor   Pel'idor ('i' as in 'fit')
Richeldis   Rikel'dis
Sarai   Sar'eye
Severan   Sev'eran ('e' as in 'set')

I

'No, lad. No, I'm not your father.'

The broad, mild-faced man in the carpenter's apron paused in his task of sweeping up the wood shavings on the workroom floor. The boy who stood in the doorway, facing him, could have been his son. They shared the same stocky figure and sandy hair, the same fresh complexion and blue eyes—the boy's blazing with hurt and indignation. He was filthy, his tunic was torn, and there was a long graze down one side of his face.

'Have you been rooting with the pigs?' the carpenter asked.

The boy took a step forward and crashed the door closed behind him.

'I fought Hal when he said I was not your son,' he said. The anger died out of his voice as he went on shakily, 'And now—you tell me it's true?'

The man set his broom against the wall and sat beside it on a bench, his hands on his knees, gazing steadily at the boy. 'Come, Owain, sit down,' he said. 'I'll tell you how it was.'

Owain moved forward and sat, not on the bench beside him, but on a stool a little way away, like a half-tamed animal that dares not come too near. He was struggling to bring his wild impatience under some sort of control. The carpenter slowly shook his head.

'Perhaps we were wrong, your mother and I,' he said. 'Perhaps we should have told you years ago. But there never seemed any need. It never seemed to matter.

'No, it didn't matter,' he added, as Owain began to protest. His voice grew sterner. 'We could have done no more for you if you had been our own son. You could have been no dearer to us. All the same, I'd rather you hadn't heard it from the lads in the street.'

Owain leaned forward, pain and eagerness together in his face.

'Please,' he begged. 'Please tell me. Who am I?'

'I don't know. At least, I can't tell you who your real parents were. But I can tell you how you came here.'

The carpenter paused briefly, and his eyes seemed fixed on something in the distance. Now Owain was too intent to break the silence. 'It was one night, nearly sixteen years ago. Your mother and I had locked up and were going to bed, when there was a knocking on the door. I thought twice about answering it; you never know what might be on your doorstep.' He smiled. 'We didn't know what was waiting out there that night.'

'And what was it?'

'A man, a tall man, all muffled up in a black cloak. And carrying some kind of bundle. He asked us for a lodging for the night. Well, I was for sending him down the street to the inn, but he said it was this house he was looking for. "You are Petroc the carpenter?" he asked me. And then the bundle he was carrying set up such a wailing, and I realised it was a baby.'

'Me?'

'You. Well, of course, your mother wouldn't hear of turning a baby away, so we let you in, you and the man in the black cloak, and your mother lit the lamps again and set out a bit of supper, and the man told us what he wanted with us.

'He'd heard me spoken of, it seems, as a steady man with no son to follow me, and he asked us if we'd take the child and bring him up as our own. Your parents were dead, he told us, and there was no one to look after you. Now, your mother was desperate for a child, for we could have none of our own, and so—well, before very long, we'd agreed to take you. The man didn't stay the night, after all. He was gone, and I heard a horse going off down the street at a furious pace. And we never saw him again.'

'But that can't be all!'

Petroc shrugged.

'We gave you your name and brought you up. We thought ourselves too lucky to ask questions.'

'But who was he? Do you think he was lying? Do you think he was my father?'

For a few moments Petroc did not answer, and

under his steady gaze Owain felt himself growing quieter. The man he had thought was his father had always been like this, slow but not stupid, thoughtful and softly-spoken. Owain curbed his impetuous questions and waited.

'At first I wondered,' Petroc went on at last. 'But now I doubt he was your father. He'd no look of you. And there was something about him—I think what he told me was the truth. Not all the truth, naturally, but the truth as far as he was willing to tell it.'

In the silence that followed, Owain wondered in a bewildered kind of way what he was to do. For fifteen years he had lived content, unquestioning, and in one sense nothing had changed. He could go on living here, busy as he had always been, learning his father's trade—and yet, Petroc was not his father. And that meant everything had changed.

'What shall I do?' he asked.

He had hardly expected an answer, but Petroc gave him one.

'Why should you do anything? Except the work you've always done.' He brought his hand down on the bench he sat on. 'You made this, and a sound piece of work it is. Remember, your mother and I have always known about you. You're no less our son because you know it now. It makes no difference.'

'It makes a difference to me.'

Petroc nodded, as if he understood, but Owain felt compelled to go on explaining himself.

'It's as if—there's somewhere, somewhere I

belong, not here. As if I was meant to be something else, and not a carpenter.'

'Our Lord was a carpenter, so they tell,' Petroc said with a smile. 'It's an honourable trade. But I can see how you feel, and I'd not force you to anything you'd no mind to.'

He gave the bench a last caress and got to his feet.

'Come through to the house.'

Owain followed him along the narrow passage that led from the workroom to their living quarters. In the kitchen the fire was dancing and Sarai, his mother, was setting plates on the scrubbed wooden table.

'You're early,' she began. 'Supper won't be…' Her voice died as she saw the look on Petroc's face. The carpenter went to her and took her hand.

'He knows,' he said.

'Oh, my dear—'

She started towards Owain and then made herself stop, as if she understood that her touch was the last thing he wanted. Instead she crossed the room to a wooden cupboard, which she unlocked with a key from the chain at her girdle. From the cupboard she took a small bundle, and spread it on the table. Owain stared down at it. There was a knitted shawl, and some fine, white baby clothes, exquisitely embroidered. And there was a leather bag closed with a silver clasp.

'These were mine?' Owain asked.

'These were what you had with you when you came to us,' Sarai told him.

Petroc picked up the bag, unclasped it, and spilled a shower of gold on to the table.

'The man who brought you left these. We'd have taken you without money, and so I told him, and we've needed no payment to bring up our own son. But I thought to keep it for you when you came of age, to set you up in your own workshop, if that was what you had a mind for.'

Stupefied, Owain stared at the table, and then at the faces of his parents.

'He was rich, the man who came?'

Petroc shrugged.

'He was some great man's messenger, that was clear enough.'

Owain put out a hand waveringly and picked up one of the coins. It did not vanish under his touch.

'I'm grateful for what you've done for me,' he said slowly, and seeing a spasm of pain cross Sarai's face he realised dimly that he could not have said anything more cruel. 'I must know who I am,' he tried to explain. 'I could take this money and travel and search—I've got to know the truth, I've got to!'

Petroc began to collect up the coins and return them to the bag. At the last he held out his hand for the one Owain still clutched, and Owain gave it to him without protest.

'I told you I could afford to bring up my own son,' Petroc said. 'And I've silver enough to send you on your travels. No need to squander your inheritance.'

Sarai drew in her breath sharply.

'But where would he go?' she asked. 'Where could he start?'

They were questions that Owain was asking himself. He was taken aback to find his needs understood so swiftly. He had expected to have to argue, perhaps even to go in defiance of his parents.

'The only way would be to trace the man who came here that night,' Petroc replied. 'I never knew his name. He was tall and dark, and he had an air about him—used to command, I could tell. But that could be said of hundreds of men. And he wore a ring—silver, with a dark stone that was engraved with a falcon's head. Fine workmanship. That would be your start, Owain, if you must go. Find the man who wears that ring.'

2

Owain paused at the top of the hill and looked back. Below him he could see the huddled roofs of the little town that until now had been his world. Dawn light was growing, reflecting pale in the river as it wound its way between the houses. A few early hearth fires sent thin columns of smoke into the still air. Owain tried and failed to distinguish the thatch of his own home.

It was the morning of the third day after his discovery that he was not Petroc's son. Although his decision to leave had been made in a rush of emotion, in hindsight he believed it was right, and he was holding to it. Petroc and Sarai both understood that he would never rest quiet until he knew the truth about himself.

So he stood on the hill-top, a leather pack on his back, and a purse at his belt generously filled with Petroc's silver. Of course he had left the town before. He had delivered goods of Petroc's making to outlying farms. And he had walked and camped in the hills with his friends. But he had never made a long journey before, and he had always known when he would return.

As he took a last farewell of the town, he thought of the journey ahead. He was bound for the court in Pelidor, to the West—one of the greatest cities in all this world of Fern, so Petroc said. There, if anywhere, he might strike the trail of the man with the falcon ring. And if the man was not his father, he could certainly tell him who was.

'I might be nobly born, I might be anyone, I might even be a king!' Owain said to himself.

Then he half smiled and shook his head, almost as embarrassed as if he had told someone else about such absurd fancies. He could not deny his hunger to know the truth about himself, but he was realistic enough not to expect to find he was anything special. And he could not hide the fact that a large part of him still wished he could go on contentedly being Owain, son of Petroc the carpenter.

Above his head, a bird began to sing. The pale sky woke into blue and gold. Owain's shadow was thrown out behind him and innumerable drops of dew glittered in the grass. He turned away from his home and pushed on with the sun at his back.

Pelidor was many days away for a solitary traveller on foot, but once he grew used to the life, Owain found that he enjoyed it. Every day there were new places and new people, every night a bed at an inn or a farmhouse. It was too early in the year to camp outdoors in comfort. And even when heavy rain caught him trudging along the road far from shelter, he consoled himself with the thought that he was drawing slowly closer to the answer to all his questions.

Gradually he realised that the countryside was changing. All his life he had been used to gentle hills and rich fields, but now his road was steadily climbing, and there were mountains on his horizon. Sometimes the road would cut through a steep cleft, with rocks shining damp on either side, streams pouring from above his head, and every crevice packed with heather and trailing fern. And it was in one of these clefts that disaster overtook him.

It was late afternoon. Owain had begun to look out for somewhere to spend the night, but for the last few miles there had been nothing. Already it was growing dark among the rocks and overhanging trees that shut out the sky. Then he heard movement ahead, and rounding a bend in the road, saw two men coming towards him. They were powerful, shabbily dressed and dark-bearded. Owain hesitated, took a few steps more in their direction, decided that he really did not like the look of them, and turned to go back. Then he stopped dead. Three others were coming up the road behind, and as he stood, undecided, a sixth dropped neatly from the rocks above and landed on the road beside him.

'Greetings,' he said, baring his teeth in what might have passed for a smile. 'Travelling alone?'

'Yes,' Owain replied, and then added quickly, 'That is, no.'

'Make your mind up, lad.' He made an elaborate pretence of looking around him. 'If you're not alone, you seem to have lost the rest of your party. That's a careless thing to do, lad, very careless. You never know who you might meet on the road. Isn't that right?'

He appealed to the other men who by this time had come up and grouped themselves in a rough circle around Owain. One or two of them grunted an assent to his question.

'You could get yourself killed,' the man went on, 'and that would be a pity.'

Owain cried out sharply as he felt his arms grasped from behind.

'No one can hear you,' the leader went on. 'Too lonely, you see. Aren't you lucky that I'm not a violent man?'

He stepped forward and as Owain struggled vainly to free himself, unfastened the purse from his belt.

'I'm doing you a favour, lad,' he smiled, weighing the purse in his hand. 'If you've nothing worth stealing, then nobody's going to bother you, see?'

It was obviously hopeless to try to fight his way out, but in the loss of the purse, Owain saw the wreckage of all his hopes of finding out who he really was. How could he go on with his journey without money? Desperately he lunged forward. The sudden movement must have surprised his captor, because he managed to wrench his arms free, and fell upon the leader, bearing him backwards to the ground. They rolled over together in the dust of the road. The leader was cursing steadily. Then Owain felt other hands grabbing him. He fought them off, only to feel himself lifted and flung backwards to the side of the road. His head struck a rock; he half rose, as if the sudden pain did not belong to him, and then crumpled up and lay still.

Water was splashing on his face. He remembered working the pump in Petroc's courtyard, filling a bucket for Sarai. Why had someone laid him under the pump? He tried to protest, but his voice came thick and unintelligible. Then he opened his eyes. He first saw hands holding a leather water-bottle, and then, dimly hovering above him, a face. A distant voice said, 'I told you he wasn't dead.'

He tried to sit up, but someone was pushing him back, and the voice, much nearer now, told him, 'Keep still. You've got a nasty cut.'

The voice knew exactly what it was about. Owain obeyed. While hands deftly bathed his

17

head, he blinked and tried to discern who the hands and voice belonged to. He realised that the dim light was not just the product of his scattered senses. It was really growing dark; in fact, someone unseen was standing close by with a torch, and in the red, uneven glow he at last managed to make sense of what was happening.

His rescuer was a girl. She had a pale face, not at all pretty, but very much alive, perhaps because of the wide, grey eyes that were intently examining his injuries. Her hair was long and honey-coloured, untidily looped up and spilling over a dark cloak and hood. The man holding the torch looked like a soldier, in a black tunic with a sword at his side. As Owain's senses returned he could hear other voices at a distance, and the movement of horses.

'That's better,' the girl said when she had finished. 'You can try to sit up now.'

Owain tried and succeeded, though his head swam alarmingly. The girl gave him the water-bottle and he drank with a grateful sigh. 'What happened?' the girl asked.

'Robbers,' Owain said thickly. 'They took—' His hand went to his belt; the purse, of course, was gone, though he still had his leather pack. He turned it out; it was empty.

'They took everything.'

A stab of fear went through him as he wondered what he was to do now.

'This is a bad road,' the girl said calmly. 'I suppose I'm lucky to have this...escort.' The pause before the word, as though she was not quite sure what to call her companions, bewildered Owain. The girl made no explanation.

'You'd better travel with us for a while,' she went on. 'Are you going far?'

'To Pelidor, lady, to the court.'

'Lady?' She smiled at Owain's belated attempt to be respectful. 'Don't call me that. My name is Richeldis. And as it happens, I'm going to Pelidor myself. I'd be glad of your company. Have you friends there?'

'No, I...'

Owain's voice trailed off. He was not sure how much of his purpose he ought to tell, or wanted to, and he felt too sick and too uncertain of the future to put it all into words. Richeldis touched his arm sympathetically.

'Don't worry. I can see you're not fit to talk. There's an inn not far ahead, so they tell me. You can rest there.'

She got to her feet and held out a hand to help Owain up. He still felt shaky, and was glad of her support.

'Very well,' Richeldis said to the soldier with the torch. 'We can go now. He will ride with us.'

The man hesitated briefly, and then strode off to where more men and horses were waiting a few yards away. They began to form up, ready to move.

'I called them my escort,' Richeldis remarked, 'but I suppose guard might be a better word. You see, in a way, I'm their prisoner.'

3

Owain's journey continued, though now he travelled on horseback, bumping along uncomfortably behind one or other of the soldiers. He wondered why, if she was a prisoner, the soldiers obeyed Richeldis, at least in the matter of allowing him to ride with them. It was some days before he found out any more. He could not talk to Richeldis while they were on the move, and in the evening, when they reached their inn, all he wanted was to crawl into bed.

The fourth night he spent with the company was also the last, so Richeldis told him, before they arrived in Pelidor. Owain's injuries were healing, and he still felt quite fresh. He ate well at supper, and afterwards joined Richeldis by the fire. The soldiers were drinking at the other side of the room, and there were few other people in the inn.

Richeldis had taken a carved wooden ball from a pocket in her cloak, and was turning it in her hands, caressing it, while she stared thoughtfully into the fire. For the first time, Owain really started to wonder about her.

'What will happen to you,' he asked, 'when we reach Pelidor?'

Richeldis looked up at him, smiling.

'I'm not sure,' she replied. 'I'll be questioned, I suppose. But there's only one question they really want the answer to, and I don't know it.' Seeing

his bewilderment, she added, 'You don't understand. I'd better explain.'

'I don't want—' Owain was beginning, but
Richeldis interrupted him.

'I'd like to tell you. I've had no one to talk to for
nearly three weeks now, and my lady always used
to say I talked too much.'

She brushed at her eyes, and Owain caught the
glitter of a tear.

'She was Lady Isolda, the White Lady. Have
you heard of her?'

Owain shook his head.

'She was the wife of Cador, the last lord of
Pelidor. My mother was Lady Isolda's waiting
woman, but she died when I was born, and my
Lady Isolda brought me up. She was the only
mother I ever knew. My father died in the war,
with Lord Cador.'

Owain felt a sudden movement of sympathy;
like him, Richeldis had never known her true parents. But she went on without giving him time to
say anything.

'You know that Pelidor is ruled by the Lord
Regent, Arven, Cador's brother? Have you ever
wondered why he is only Lord Regent, not Lord in
his own right?'

Owain shook his head. His home town was so
remote from Pelidor that goings-on at the court
had never seemed very important, and even if he
had heard the names Richeldis mentioned, they
meant very little to him.

'Lady Isolda had a child,' Richeldis went on.
'At about the time she heard that Lord Cador was

dead in the war. And she was afraid that Arven might kill the child, so that he could rule. So she sent the baby away, to be brought up in secret, and she would not tell Arven where he was.'

Owain found his head suddenly whirling. A child sent away to be brought up in secret—another child turning up mysteriously at the house of Petroc the carpenter. Owain remembered the day he had left home, and his ambitions of discovering noble birth and a heritage for himself. But not this... No! He shrank away from the coincidence, kept quiet, and Richeldis, intent on her story, noticed nothing.

'Arven isn't an evil man,' she went on. 'And he dared not kill my lady, even if he had wanted to, because everyone loved her, and they would have rebelled against him if he had harmed her. But he kept her a virtual prisoner on her own estates, north of here, while he did all he could to find the child.'

'And did he?'

'No.' Richeldis paused, took a deep breath, and went on, 'And now my lady is dead, and perhaps her secret has died with her.'

At first, Owain thought that she was going to give way to tears. She sat with averted head, and then after a moment pushed back her hair and turned to face him again.

'She had a fall while she was riding,' she explained. 'I was nearest to her, and I went to her, but she died a moment later. And now Arven wants to question me, because if she told anyone what she had done with her child, she would have told me. And I was with her when she died, and if she had kept her secret until then, she might have told me in the end.'

'But she didn't?' Owain asked.

'No. She always said that I would know when the time was right. I always thought she meant when her son was grown up and it was safe to acknowledge him. And when she was dying...there wasn't time. She said, "My daughter...," that was all. It's what I was to her, but she never told me about her real child.'

Owain felt chilled, for all the warmth of the fire.

'But if Arven thinks you know...'

'He might make life difficult for me.' Her lips tightened. 'I suppose I shall have to face that.'

Admiring her courage, Owain asked, 'Then what will he do?'

'I don't know. The Council in Pelidor will not acknowledge him as Lord while they have any hope of finding Lord Cador's heir. And Arven has a son of his own he would like to succeed him.' She sighed and went on, 'Sooner or later, I suppose, the Council will have to accept the fact that the child is lost.'

'And they'll make Arven Lord?'

Owain spoke indignantly, surprised at how strongly he felt when he had never heard this story until now.

Richeldis smiled faintly.

'We could do worse than Arven. I told you, he isn't evil, he wouldn't enjoy doing wrong. He might be prepared to kill a child who stood in his way, but as Regent he hasn't done badly. He's efficient, and just as he sees justice. But that's not the most important thing….'

Her voice trailed off. Owain made an encouraging noise.

'You know that Fern is only one of the Six Worlds—and the most remote?'

Owain nodded.

'Have you ever seen any of the ships that come from Centre?'

'No.'

'Nor have I. Nor has anyone in Pelidor, because Arven has forbidden them to come. I've even met people who don't believe in them any more. After all, ships that fly through the air—ships that fly from world to world! Stupid, isn't it?'

She leaned forward earnestly.

'But on Centre they know how to send the ships, and they would come and bring us trade and news and new ideas. And they used to bring the priests of the Lord who were trained on Centre to teach the rest of us—but Arven doesn't want that. He sees it all as a threat to his power, and to Fern. He really believes that it's best for Fern to have nothing to do with the other worlds. And he won't recognise any power, even God's power, above his own. He has forbidden the ships, and banished the priests of God, and other lords do the same because they're afraid of the power of Pelidor. And if Arven's son succeeds him, we could lose the link with Centre and the other worlds for ever. We could go back to being barbarians.'

She fell silent. Owain slowly digested everything that he had heard, awestruck because, if he really was Cador's heir it would be his job to do something about it, to persuade the Council to accept him, to unseat Arven, and to forge a new link with Centre so that Fern should not be lost from the fellowship of the Six Worlds. It's nonsense, he comforted himself, I'm a carpenter's apprentice, I can't be expected to mend a whole world.

Richeldis had turned back to the fire and taken up again the carved wooden ball that she had let rest in her lap, turning it in the firelight and tracing the patterns with her fingers. Owain really looked at it for the first time, and felt himself turn to stone. He had seen it before.

Or if not that one, then one like it. Petroc made them. There were several balls, all intricately carved, nesting one inside the other. Petroc fashioned them lovingly, as toys for children, not very many of them, because they took a long time and they were expensive. Owain could not do such fine work yet.

'Richeldis...' he said.

She looked up at him.

'Where did you get that?'

'The ball? I've always had it. I suppose my lady gave it to me. It's beautiful, isn't it?'

She handed it to him, and he turned it in his fingers, admiring the familiar carving, the leaves and flowers and heads of tiny animals. The smaller balls moved softly inside. Owain knew he had to make his mind up. He could have ignored Richeldis' tale, dismissed it as something that had very little to do with him, until now. For this ball was a direct link between Petroc the carpenter and the household of Lady Isolda. Because he had seen it, Owain could not disregard the evidence of who he was.

'Richeldis,' he began nervously, 'listen. There's something I have to tell you....'

4

In the late afternoon of the following day, Owain had his first sight of Pelidor. They had been travelling through forest, and under the shadow of the trees it was already growing dark. Then they broke out into meadowland. Ahead, the road looped around the foot of a hill, following the line of a great wall, and then led to a gateway flanked with watchtowers. Owain could see line after line of roofs, crowded together up the slopes of the hill, and at the summit, the towers of a citadel standing out crisply against the sky. Beyond the city the sun was going down in a sky barred with cloud.

Owain let out a long breath.

'Pelidor,' said the soldier he was riding with. 'You've not seen it before, lad?'

'No.'

'It's a fine place.'

What would he have said, Owain wondered, if

he knew that he was sharing his horse with Pelidor's heir? For after his talk with Richeldis on the previous night, he had to accept that he was Pelidor's heir. Richeldis, between shock, wonder and even a little amusement, had not questioned his story or the evidence of the carved wooden ball. All Owain wanted to know was what was going to happen now.

'We can't just walk in and announce you,' Richeldis had said. 'There'll be danger from Arven. Better go quietly and see how things stand. And then—'

She had broken off, disturbed by the movement of the soldiers at the other side of the room.

'They'll wonder what we're finding to talk about,' she warned. 'There's more I need to ask you, but it will have to wait. For now, say nothing to anyone.'

Owain was relieved at her advice, and quite content to remain in the guise of a humble visitor to the great city. He looked around him with interest as they reached the gateway, and passed through and along a steep street leading straight up towards the citadel.

'This is the Street of the Councillors,' his soldier informed him. 'Each of the Lords Councillors has his own estates, but they all keep a house in this street as well. You can see their arms over the doors.'

Owain had already noticed that each doorway was surmounted by a shield, the devices picked out in colours that blazed against the grey stonework.

'Why do they do that?' he asked.

'To show that they're lords in their own right, lad, and not just servants of Pelidor. And the Lord of Pelidor himself can't rule without their consent.'

Owain found that interesting. He remembered what Richeldis had said about the Council. And he remembered his own lord, Kynan, at home. Once, Petroc had carved him a magnificent chair for his great hall. Owain wondered if Kynan recalled the scruffy apprentice who had helped deliver the chair, and, if so, what he would feel if the same scruffy apprentice should present himself in Pelidor, claiming to be the lost heir. And then he found himself passing through the gate of the citadel, and there was no time for further wondering.

He slid quickly to the ground and went to the bridle of Richeldis' horse, holding it so she could dismount.

'Thank you,' she said, and murmured in a low voice, 'Stay with me. Let me do the talking.'

With a deep breath she picked up her skirts and advanced across the courtyard. Daylight was fading, but the torches were not yet lit, and the open doorway gaped like a dark cavern. No one came to direct them, but Richeldis did not hesitate. Up a flight of steps, down a dim passageway, and into a wide hall where the only light came from windows high in the walls, the golden light of sunset splashing down onto grey flagstones, while in the corners shadows hung like cobwebs. Opposite the door where they had entered, a staircase led up into darkness. Owain shivered.

Richeldis paused and looked around her. At first it seemed as if the hall was empty.

'I expected another escort,' she admitted. 'And perhaps not so courteous as the first one. Now, I don't know....'

Her voice died away irresolutely. Owain moved forward, looking around him, and realised that they were not, after all, alone. In a recess at the other side of the hall was a table, and someone seated at it, his head resting on his hand. His face was hidden, but there was something in his posture that suggested utter weariness. He might have been part of the shadows, for he was dressed in black, and the bent head was dark. There was a scatter of papers on the table, but without a lamp Owain guessed it would be impossible to read or write.

Obviously their arrival had gone unnoticed. Owain touched Richeldis' arm, drawing her attention to the silent presence, but before either of them could move the silence was shattered by the ringing of spurred boots on stone, and a young man came clattering down the stairs. His arrival seemed to set the shadows flying. He was tall and broad-shouldered, with a shock of tawny hair, and he wore a scarlet tunic laced with gold.

'Lights! Lights!' he was bellowing as he reached the foot of the stairs. 'Lights in this god-forsaken hole!'

He stood still, gazing around him as if he was conscious of the splendid figure he cut.

'Jerold,' Richeldis whispered. 'My Lord Arven's son. A lout.'

Already a scurry of servants had begun to appear and set torches in brackets around the hall.

Light spread, but no one noticed Owain and Richeldis standing unobtrusively beside the outer door. Jerold strode across the hall to the table.

'Hilarion!'

The seated figure raised his head. Owain felt shocked; this was a boy no older than himself, but the expression on the still, pale face had the reserve of a much older man.

'My Lord?'

'Stand when you address me!'

Hilarion inclined his head slightly and rose, with one hand on the table as if he needed the support.

'I want the Master of Horse. Have you seen him?'

'No, my Lord.'

'Then go and find him!'

Hilarion groped behind his chair and produced an ebony cane; as he moved away from the table, Owain realised that he leaned heavily on it, walking with a limp. He was not sure what happened next. There was a scuffle, the cane went ringing across the floor, and Hilarion fell, crumpling into a dark heap at Jerold's feet. Jerold let out a great shout of laughter. Owain started forward, only to feel Richeldis' hand round his wrist as she breathed out, 'No!'

The movement at last drew Jerold's attention to them. He paced across the hall towards them, a smile curling his lips.

'And who might you be?' he asked.

Richeldis drew herself up.

'I am Richeldis, waiting woman to my Lady

Isolda, the White Lady. Here at the request of my Lord Regent, Arven.'

Jerold's face twitched at the word 'Regent'. His smile became cruel.

'Well, little Richeldis,' he drawled. 'I remember you.'

He reached out and twisted a strand of Richeldis' hair around his finger. She did not move. Jerold was looking down at her with an expression that for some reason made Owain bristle, but he had sense enough to keep quiet.

'We must see what we can find to amuse you in Pelidor,' Jerold said.

Richeldis did not reply directly.

'Perhaps you would inform your father I am here.'

Jerold gave her hair a vicious jerk, and released her.

'I'm no servant,' he snapped, and strode off down a side passage.

The tug must have hurt, but Richeldis' expression did not change, except for a tightening of the lips.

'As I said, a lout. He's made some progress since he used to pull the wings off flies, but not much.'

'Lady Richeldis.'

The quiet voice drew their attention back to Hilarion, who stood a pace or two away, armoured in such frosty dignity that the ugly incident they had witnessed might never have taken place.

'Forgive me, Lady,' he said. 'I was told to watch

for your coming. If you follow me, I'll take you to my Lord Arven.'

He moved away awkwardly across the hall, but before they reached the foot of the stairs, another man appeared above them. He was tall, his dark hair winged with silver, and he too wore black, unrelieved except for a broad silver chain stretching from shoulder to shoulder. Petroc's words suddenly came back to Owain: a tall dark man with an air about him, used to command. But when Owain looked at his hands, he wore no ring at all, much less one carved with a falcon's head.

'Richeldis,' he said, smiling. 'You're welcome to Pelidor. Come with me. Very well, Hilarion,' he added. 'You can go. Don't wait for me.'

Hilarion nodded and drew back. As he looked up and the older man looked down, Owain was struck by the likeness in the faces, and realised that the two must be father and son. But how did that explain the expression in Hilarion's eyes, that he could only describe as one of sick despair?

Hastily Owain pulled himself together and followed Richeldis and the dark man up the stairs and down a long, panelled corridor. Light spilled from an open door at the end. The dark man stood aside and motioned Richeldis to enter. Owain swallowed, and realised his hands were clenched. Deliberately making himself relax, he followed Richeldis into the room.

5

There was one man in the room, standing with his back to the fire, but Owain felt that if the room had been thronged with people, he would still have noticed no one else. He was tall and bony, with a slight forward stoop. His face was commandingly ugly, the nose jutting, the eyes deep-set. He had rust-coloured hair, peppered with grey, and he wore a rust-coloured tunic. Owain did not need to be told that this was the Lord Regent, Arven.

'Come in, girl, sit down,' he said brusquely, as Richeldis entered. 'No one's going to bite you.'

Richeldis could not have looked less as if she expected to be bitten—or cared if she was. She dropped Arven a deep curtsey, and then composedly took her seat close to the fire.

'And who's this?' Piercing eyes under bushy eyebrows were fixed on Owain. 'Who's the boy?'

'He is my attendant,' Richeldis explained.

'I've never seen him before.'

'We met on the road.' Richeldis seemed quite untroubled by Arven's manner. She glanced sideways at Owain and her lips quirked into a smile. 'He was on his way to seek his fortune in Pelidor. And since, my Lord,' she went on more incisively, 'your men forced me from my Lady's house with no one to attend me and with scarcely a change of clothing, I should think—'

'Very well, very well,' Arven interrupted. He seemed suddenly to be in a better mood; Owain wondered if many people stood up to him as Richeldis did. 'I suppose we can feed one more mouth.'

He waved dismissively at Owain, who moved to stand behind Richeldis' chair, hoping that was the correct thing to do, and hoping also that he would not be sent away. He breathed more freely when Arven, apparently losing interest in him, spoke to the dark man who still stood beside the door.

'Come in, Severan, sit down. No ceremony. I want you to hear this.'

Severan bowed slightly, closed the door and took the seat Arven indicated, opposite Richeldis. From where he stood, Owain had a good view of him, though he could see nothing but the top of Richeldis' head.

'I was grieved to hear of your Lady's death,' Arven began.

Richeldis evidently did not think that required a response.

'She will be much missed,' the Regent added.

But not by you, Owain thought, and almost spoke his thought aloud.

'Did she say anything before she died?'

'Nothing that could possibly interest you, my Lord,' Richeldis replied calmly.

'But she said something!' Arven was leaning forward now, his eagerness undisguised. 'Tell me what it was.'

Richeldis hesitated, and when she spoke there was a quiver in her voice.

'She said, "My daughter...." It is how she thought of me.'

34

'But she said nothing of her own child?'

Richeldis shook her head.

'No, my Lord.'

Arven drew back again, baffled, and it was Severan who took up the questioning, though his aquiline features showed little of what he was feeling.

'You know, my dear, don't you, of Lady Isolda's own child?'

'I know there was such a child, my Lord.'

'He will be as old as you now, almost of age and almost ready to take command in Pelidor.'

A pause; Richeldis waited.

'Lady Isolda told you nothing of him?'

'No, my Lord.'

'Severan—'

Arven was interrupting again, but a quick glance from Severan silenced him. Owain decided that Severan, though a servant, could well be the more dangerous man.

'And she gave you no idea of where this young man will be now?' he went on smoothly.

Again Richeldis shook her head.

'The ring, Severan,' Arven said testily. 'Ask her about the ring.'

Owain pricked his ears up at the mention of a ring, but realised a moment later that it had nothing to do with him.

'You know that when he ruled in Pelidor, Lord Cador wore a ring?' Severan asked. 'A ring that has been worn by the Lords of Pelidor for generations. And when he rode to the war, he left this ring with the Lady Isolda. But no one has seen it since. Have you seen it?'

'No, my Lord.'

Arven made an impatient sound, and shifted restlessly. His patience was wearing thin in the face of Richeldis' persistent, calm denials.

'It was a ruby,' he said. 'A ruby set in gold. Did she wear it? Did you find it after she died?'

'No—but she said one thing to me.'

'Yes?'

'That she had given the ring of Pelidor to Pelidor's heir.'

Arven gave an exasperated snort and began to pace up and down. Severan, for his part, stayed calm, and a faintly enigmatic smile touched his lips.

'So if we find the young man, we find the ring,' he mused. 'A pretty puzzle your Lady set us. And you can tell us no more?'

This time Richeldis' denial was scarcely necessary, and he scarcely waited for it before continuing.

'My dear girl, you must be tired and hungry after your journey. We'll keep you no longer for this time. I hope you'll enjoy your stay in Pelidor. And if you should happen to remember anything that has...shall we say, escaped your memory at the moment, you will tell us right away?'

Once again he scarcely waited for Richeldis' reply before going to the door and summoning a servant. Richeldis rose and curtsied again to both men. Severan ordered the servant to take her to her room. As Owain followed, he was rather surprised that the interview had been so pleasant.

He was also surprised at the pleasant rooms that had been prepared for Richeldis, high in one of the towers of the citadel. There was a bedroom, and a comfortably furnished sitting room, where a meal was already set out. Richeldis sent away the servant, saying that Owain would attend her, but once they were alone, she invited him to sit at the table, and sat down herself with a great sigh.

'So that's over!'

'It wasn't so bad,' Owain remarked.

Richeldis laughed.

'Don't you believe it! That was only the beginning. Severan isn't stupid.'

'Who is he?'

'Lord Arven's steward. And quite competent to rule Pelidor single-handed. Hilarion, that we met in the hall, is his son—but I suppose you could see that.'

Owain nodded, and said, 'I thought at first he might be the man I'm looking for—the one who wore the falcon ring.'

Richeldis looked astonished at the idea.

'My Lady would never have trusted Severan. He used to serve Lord Cador, but when he died, he went straight over to Arven. In an odd sort of way, I trust Arven—at least you know where you stand with him. But no one in their right mind would trust Severan.'

'You've met him before?' Owain asked.

'He came to visit my Lady once or twice. To find out what he could learn, I suppose. She wouldn't tell him anything.'

She began to investigate the supper dishes; there was bread, chicken in a savoury sauce, fruit and wine, all served generously enough to feed Owain as well.

'Let's make the most of it,' Richeldis said. 'We don't know how long it's going to last. You were listening, I suppose?' she asked. 'You heard what Severan said—and what he didn't? This is the bribe. This, and these rooms, and anything else I like to ask for, I expect, while I try to remember whatever it was that "escaped my memory". If I don't remember, things might get more unpleasant. So we'd better decide what we're going to do.'

She attacked her food enthusiastically, and signed to Owain to do the same. He did so, but he could think as well as eat, and after a while he asked, 'Did you tell them the truth?'

Richeldis gazed at him, wide-eyed.

'Would I tell a lie? Every word I said was the exact truth, and I held nothing back. Just as well they only wanted to know what my Lady told me. They didn't ask if I know where Pelidor's heir is now, or if I just happened to pick him up on the road!'

She giggled appreciatively. Owain felt less amused.

'What was all that about a ring?' he asked.

'That's something I meant to ask you. What I said was true: my Lady told me she had given the ring of Pelidor to Pelidor's heir. So you should have it.'

She looked at him enquiringly. Owain's mind was a blank.

'I've never set eyes on it.'

Richeldis frowned.

'That doesn't make sense. My Lady wouldn't lie. She smiled when she said it, as if she knew she was setting everyone a riddle, but she wouldn't lie. You must have it.'

'But I haven't. My f—, that is, Petroc showed me everything that was with me when I came to him. There was no ring.'

'Would he have sold it?'

'No!'

His protest drew a smile from Richeldis.

'Don't be so touchy. I'm not suggesting Petroc stole it. But perhaps he had great need of money— perhaps for you. Did he ever—'

'No, it's not possible,' Owain interrupted. 'Petroc is a prosperous man, a master craftsman. Besides, there was money, a whole bag of gold pieces. If there had ever been a ring, he would have told me.' Richeldis gave a vexed shake of her head.

'My Lady's puzzle is harder than it looks. And we need that ring. If you had it, you could present yourself in front of the Council. Without it, they're hardly likely to believe you.'

'There's one person who might know where it is—the man who took me to Petroc.'

'The man with the falcon ring.' Richeldis sniffed disparagingly. 'Another ring, and we don't know where that one is, either! We—'

She broke off at the sound of a light tap on the door, and, exchanging a glance with Owain, called, 'Come in!'

The door opened; Hilarion was standing on the threshold.

'I came to see if you have everything you want, Lady,' he explained.

'Everything's lovely, thank you,' Richeldis answered, and suddenly went on, 'Have you had supper? Why don't you come and join us?'

She held out a hand towards him. Hilarion moved hesitantly forward, and then seemed to recollect himself.

'No, Lady, I...forgive me, I have duties.'

He withdrew, clumsy in his haste. When he had gone, Richeldis remained silent, gazing meditatively at the closed door.

'What's the matter?' Owain asked.

'I could have done without that!'

'You invited him in,' Owain said, not understanding.

'Yes, making the best of it. I don't want to seem as if I've got anything to hide. But you're supposed to be my servant, and I wish he hadn't seen us with our heads together. I don't know anything against him, but he is Severan's son.'

They looked at each other and continued their meal in an uneasy silence.

6

Richeldis' complaint about being forced to leave home without a change of clothing must have been noticed, for the next day, after breakfast, she was visited by one of the court dressmakers. In Owain's opinion, she showed an unreasonable interest in what she was to wear, and as far as he could see, she was settled for the rest of the day. He slid out.

For a while he explored the corridors of the citadel, and soon came to an outer door. It led into a garden, a peaceful place, almost wild, with narrow paths that wound between shrubbery. The ground was roughly terraced, following the slopes of the hill. Feeling the need of a quiet place to think, Owain went out and found himself a seat beside a pool, under an enormous tree, from where he could look across the walls of the citadel and the roofs of Pelidor, out into the distance that was lost in a haze. Somewhere out there was his home and everything he was familiar with. He was tempted for a moment to walk out of the gate and take the road that would lead him back there.

Knowing it was impossible, he was trying to think of a more practical course of action when he was disturbed by the sound of someone approaching along the path. He sprang to his feet. He was not sure he should be there, and he did not want to explain himself. There were enough places to hide; he was not sure afterwards what made him choose the tree. But it was a good tree for climbing. Almost without thinking, he placed one foot in a knot in the trunk, grabbed at a branch overhead, and hauled himself upwards. Then he lay along the length of the branch and looked down.

The newcomer was Hilarion. He made his way slowly along the path, leaning on his cane, and to Owain's dismay settled himself on the bench that Owain had just left. Owain was even more dismayed when he took a book out of the pocket of his robe and began to read.

He could be there all day! he thought.

He would feel an idiot dropping out of the tree, and he would have even more to explain. But the thought of staying there until Hilarion had finished studying his book was even more irksome. The decision was taken out of his hands as he heard the footsteps of a third person—rapid footsteps this time, from the other direction.

It was Jerold. He was dressed for riding, striding along and slapping a whip against his leg as he walked. If he had looked up, he could have seen Owain in the tree, but he did not look up. They never do, Owain thought smugly.

Jerold came to an abrupt stop as he saw Hilarion, and roughly snatched the book from his hands. Owain heard Hilarion's gasp of protest, immediately suppressed.

'What's that?' Jerold asked.

He riffled contemptuously through the pages and then stood weighing the book in his hand, watching Hilarion with an unpleasant grin on his face.

'Do you want it back?' he asked.

'If you please, my Lord.'

Hilarion had not risen from the bench; he sat erect, his hands tightly clenched.

'What will you do to get it?'

When Hilarion did not reply, Jerold took a step back, holding the book up, above the pool. At that, Hilarion came to his feet.

'Don't!'

The single word, sharp with fear, made Jerold laugh softly.

'Kneel down, then, there, on the path, and ask me for it. And I just might give it to you—if you do it nicely.'

Owain could see that Hilarion was shaking. His face was white and desperate; he was close to breaking point. Somehow Owain did not want to see him humiliated.

'Go on, kneel!'

Jerold was holding the book out, over the water, beneath Owain's branch. As he raised it a little higher, Owain snaked an arm down and twitched it out of his grasp.

Jerold looked up, gaping.

'Good morning, my Lord,' Owain said agreeably.

'Give me that!'

'No.'

Baffled fury had driven astonishment from Jerold's face.

'Do you want me to take it?'

Owain smiled.

'Try.'

He was just in the mood for a fight, and felt

rather regretful, as Jerold took a step back, to realise he would not have one.

'I wouldn't soil my hands on a servant,' Jerold said, trying, and failing, to sound contemptuous. He retreated further down the path. 'I'll have you whipped for insolence!' he threatened, shouting, as he disappeared among the trees.

Owain slid from the branch, swung, and dropped neatly to the ground at Hilarion's side.

'Your book, my Lord.'

He held it out, but Hilarion did not take it. He was gazing at Owain, white-faced and furious.

'You did *not* have to interfere!'

'Would you rather have had a wet book?'

'He would have given it to me.'

Owain shrugged. It was hardly worth arguing.

'I could have handled it. I don't need protection from him!'

Bowing slightly, Owain held out the book without a word. Hilarion took it and turned away, reaching for the cane which he had left resting against the bench. Then his shoulders sagged.

'I'm sorry.'

Suddenly he sounded young, and very miserable.

'That's all right.' Owain grinned. 'I enjoyed it. I don't suppose he's ever been quite so surprised.'

He was rewarded by seeing Hilarion smile faintly. Hilarion sat down, and after a moment's hesitation, Owain sat beside him.

'Is the book very precious?' he asked.

Hilarion caressed the cover.

'Any book is precious,' he replied. 'There are none made on Fern, except for a few that are copied—I've done copying myself. All the printing presses are on Centre, and that's where this came from. And now Lord Arven won't let the ships come, we can't get any more. This is my father's.'

'What is it?'

Hilarion opened the book at the title page. 'The Sayings of our Lord,' Owain read.

'It's everything that men remember about what our Lord told us,' Hilarion explained, and added diffidently, 'I used to think it made sense of everything. But now...I don't know. Our Lord lived so long ago, and on another world, our home world, not even on Centre. So long, and so far away.' He shivered. 'I can't believe any more that he cares about us here on Fern.'

Owain found himself suddenly looking down into a pit of despair. He did not know what to say.

'And if that weren't enough,' Hilarion went on, a thread of energy creeping back into his voice, 'Lord Arven cuts us off from Centre and the other worlds because he's afraid of losing his power. Afraid! While Fern rots.'

'You should talk to Richeldis,' Owain said. 'That is, my Lady,' he corrected himself, Hilarion's raised brows reminding him that this was a very unmannerly way of speaking for the servant he was supposed to be. 'She was saying the same thing.'

'And there's nothing any of us can do.' He reached out towards Owain. 'Did you ever see one of the ships from Centre?' Owain shook his head. 'I did—when I was very small. It must have been one of the last. I remember my father lifting me up and showing me. It was...beautiful. A silver arrow, soaring—free.'

He made a sudden movement of disgust, as if reminded too powerfully of his own crippled, earthbound body. The movement knocked his cane to the ground. Owain started to retrieve it for him and then checked, letting Hilarion do it himself. He got to his feet, smiling rather bitterly.

'Shall we walk?' Hilarion suggested.

'If you want to.'

'I'll show you where you can pick some flowers for your Lady.'

The idea had never occurred to Owain, but he felt it was a good one, particularly as he had vanished for most of the morning. They walked down the path, Owain suiting his pace to Hilarion's slower one.

'I have a message for your Lady,' Hilarion said after a moment. 'You may as well deliver it. She's invited tonight to dine with my Lord Arven, in his private apartments.'

'A great honour,' Owain murmured.

Hilarion had not missed the hint of sarcasm.

'It is, in Arven's eyes,' he asserted. 'Listen—' He stopped, and grasped Owain's arm. 'Tell her—tell her if she knows anything, not to hide it. If she does as Arven tells her, they'll treat her well. If not...' His eyes were desperate again. His grip on Owain's arm tightened. 'If not, they'll make her speak, somehow, Arven and my father.'

7

Owain was not present at Arven's dinner that evening, but he waited in Richeldis' rooms for her to come back. She looked tired; he had never seen her discouraged, but she clearly had something on her mind.

'What happened?' Owain asked.

Richeldis sank into a chair, kicked off her shoes and pulled off the ribbon that restrained her hair.

'Nothing happened,' she replied. 'But a great deal was said. Arven tells me that in seven days' time there'll be a meeting of the Lords Councillors. He would like to make a statement to them concerning the succession of Pelidor.'

Owain did not need any prompting to make sense of that.

'He expects you to tell him?'

'Yes. He was warning me, very politely, that I've got seven days—or less—to make my mind up. You know,' she added, smiling, 'in seven days exactly, it's my birthday. *Not* the way I should choose to spend it!'

Owain was amazed that she could take it so lightly. 'You shouldn't stay here,' he said, frightened on her behalf. 'Go, before he harms you.'

Richeldis looked up at him.

'Go? Where?'

'Go to Petroc.' The idea had just come to him, but on reflection, it was a good one. 'No one would look for you there. And Petroc and Sarai would welcome you.'

After a moment's surprise, Richeldis nodded thoughtfully.

'Maybe. But how would I get there? In any case,' she added, more energetically, 'I don't want to run away. I want to stay and see you in your right place, as ruler of Pelidor. And it looks as if I have seven days to do it.'

So far Owain had not had time to tell her about his encounter that morning with Hilarion, but now he described what had happened, and was pleased to see her looking interested.

'We can't go on like this,' he said. 'We have to ask someone for help. Hilarion might know who wears the falcon ring.'

'Can we trust him?' Richeldis asked.

'I think so. He wants to serve God, if he can. He said just what you said about losing touch with Centre. And he doesn't support Arven.'

Richeldis frowned.

'But he is Severan's son. What he said could have been a trick to win your confidence. Severan is capable of it, believe me. All right,' she added, as Owain began to protest. 'I wasn't there, I didn't hear him, but all the same....'

Her voice died away. She sat silent for a moment, and then got briskly to her feet.

'I'm going to bed,' she announced. 'We'll talk to Hilarion in the morning. You're right, we have to do something.'

Owain slept badly, but when he got up the next morning he felt relieved to think of taking action.

So he might have known, he reflected, that action would be impossible, because he could not find Hilarion. The steward's son presumably had his own duties, and Richeldis had warned Owain not to ask for him directly.

By the end of the morning he was thoroughly frustrated.

'Never mind,' Richeldis said. 'Go to the kitchen and beg some food for us. It's a lovely day, we'll eat in the garden. He might be there again.'

'I've already looked.'

He obeyed Richeldis, however, and they were rewarded not much later, when, walking through the garden with a couple of well-filled napkins, they came upon Hilarion, bent over his book on the same bench by the pool and the tree. He slid the book away and rose to his feet as they approached.

'Hello,' Richeldis said. 'Owain told me it was beautiful out here, so I had to come and see for myself. Thank you for the flowers.'

Hilarion murmured something inaudible and looked as if he would withdraw.

'Don't let us chase you away,' Richeldis protested, putting out a hand to stop him. 'Stay and eat with us—please.'

As Hilarion hesitated Owain realised that part of his trouble was an overwhelming shyness. But after a moment's struggle he sat down again, and Richeldis, seating herself at the other end of the bench, covered his diffidence with a flow of chatter as she set out the food on napkins, arranging bread and cheese as if it were a queen's feast. Owain squatted on the grass at their feet.

'I remember you came with your father to visit my Lady Isolda,' Richeldis said. 'I was just learning to ride, and you spent the whole afternoon schooling the horse, or me, or both of us.'

Hilarion smiled faintly.

'Yes, I remember.'

'You ride very well. Who taught you?'

'My father. He taught me to ride and to swim and to use a sword. He always said—' Hilarion paused, colouring slightly, and then went on, 'He said just because of this foot, I shouldn't spend my whole life like an invalid.'

Something about that gave Owain a new light on Severan. He had thought of the steward always as Arven's shadow, a clever plotter, with a mind but no heart. Now he realised that at least he cared for his son; the bond between them was more complicated than he had thought.

'That sounds very wise,' Richeldis said. 'You must love him very much.'

Hilarion averted his head.

'I hate him.'

Richeldis reached out and touched his shoulder, but he seemed unaware of it.

'It used to be different,' he went on. 'Once, we used to live in the Street of the Councillors—my father sits on the Council, you know, not as a full member, but to advise, and make a record. And he—' He broke off.

'And when you lived there—' Richeldis prompted gently.

'Everything was different. And then two years ago, when my mother died, the house was closed up and we came to live here in the court. And since then... I suppose before, I was too young to realise that my father is a traitor.'

He was talking freely now. Owain had been surprised how quickly the conversation had progressed, but he could understand Hilarion's need, at last, to share the black thoughts that he lived with every day.

'A traitor to Pelidor?' Richeldis asked.

Her eyes had signalled clearly to Owain, 'Let me handle this.'

'A traitor to all that Pelidor used to stand for,' Hilarion replied. 'I thought he believed in friendship with Centre and the rest of the Six Worlds, and in the God who made all worlds. He taught me—but it was all hypocrisy. He follows Arven!'

'And you—'

'I wish the ships would come again. But what can I do, alone? I've prayed, but God doesn't listen to me.'

'How do you know?' Richeldis asked.

Hilarion looked bewildered. 'If he listened, he would answer me. He would do something.'

'Hilarion, sometimes we have to wait for God's answer.'

Hilarion looked as if he was about to argue, but he said nothing. He shook his head slightly, not as if he was rejecting what Richeldis said, but as if he found it difficult to think about. Richeldis exchanged a glance with Owain, and Owain understood that she had made her decision.

'Hilarion,' she began, 'you were at Arven's dinner last night. Did you hear what he said to me?'

'No.'

'He told me that in seven days' time—six days, now—he wants to report to the Lords Councillors about the succession. He wants me to tell him what to say.' She had all Hilarion's attention now, and she began choosing her next words very carefully. 'Hilarion, I'm afraid that if—'

Before she could say more, she was interrupted by a confused shouting, faint because of distance, but growing closer. There was the sound of running footsteps, and a door crashed open not far off. Owain sprang to his feet. At first he could see nothing, but then approaching through the garden came a little knot of the guard. Two of them held pinioned a smaller man, shabbily dressed, who was struggling wildly. At the head of the column was Jerold, his face savage with triumph. He strode towards the citadel, passing not far from the bench, but not noticing the three who watched there. Owain dashed down the path and grabbed at the last of the soldiers as he went by.

'What is it?' he gasped. 'What's going on?'

The guard paused.

'He's a spy, lad,' he explained. 'Lord Jerold spotted him, down in the city. Looks as if he's a spy from Centre.'

8

The soldier pulled away from Owain's grasp and hurried after the others. Owain turned back to Richeldis. She and Hilarion had heard what the soldier had said, and were already on their feet.

'A spy from Centre!' Richeldis repeated. 'Hilarion, what will they do to him?'

'I'm not sure...question him, of course. Maybe they'll kill him.'

'Then we've got to stop them!'

Hilarion shook his head helplessly.

'There's nothing we can do.'

'We can try.'

She set off, running, along the path the soldiers had taken. Owain, biting back furious impatience, waited for Hilarion.

'No—go with her,' Hilarion said. 'Go on, I'll follow.'

Released, Owain caught Richeldis up at the door to the citadel. They sped down a passage, through another door, and found themselves in the hall where they had waited on their arrival in Pelidor. The soldiers were drawn up there, still holding their prisoner, who had stopped struggling and stood quiet, except for his eyes, that darted restlessly back and forth. Owain could see his fear.

Jerold was halfway up the stairs, shouting, Owain thought, fit to wake the dead.

'Father! Severan! Come here!'

Arven appeared at the head of the stairs, with

Severan a pace or two behind. His impatient rebuke at the noise died away as Jerold clattered down into the hall again, grasped the prisoner's shoulder and flung him to his knees on the stone floor.

'A spy, Father! A spy from Centre!'

Arven came down after his son and stood in silence, inspecting the man crouched in front of him. Severan followed.

'How do we know what he is?' he enquired, a certain cat-like disdain in his face and voice. 'He has confessed?'

'He doesn't need to confess!' Jerold grabbed a canvas bag that one of the soldiers was holding and thrust it into Severan's hands. 'Look at that! Books! New books from Centre. And this.'

The object he handed over was smaller. Severan took it, letting the bag of books slide to the floor, and Owain edged a little closer, trying to see what it was.

'Interesting,' Severan remarked.

Dangling from his hand on a leather thong was a wooden cross.

'Interesting!' Jerold burst out. 'Is that all you've got to say?'

'You do not find it interesting, my Lord?'

Jerold swung his head from side to side, baffled by the delicate mockery in Severan's tone. 'It's evidence, that's what it is,' he said. 'It's the sign of that false god they worship on Centre. It was forbidden here when the priests were banished. It shows this fellow is up to no good.'

'Undoubtedly,' Severan agreed. 'And that is why I find it most interesting.'

All this time Arven had not spoken, but now he turned to Severan.

'He's from Centre,' he said. 'Or what he carries comes from there. And I want to know where he was taking it. Here, you, fellow, get on your feet.'

The prisoner obeyed shrinkingly, his glance flickering from Arven to Severan and back again.

'Who sent you here?' Arven asked abruptly. 'Are you from Centre?'

The man did not reply.

'Where were you going? To someone in Pelidor?'

Again the man kept silence.

'Father, I could make him—' Jerold began, eagerly.

Arven quietened him with an irritated gesture. He leaned forward, bringing his face close to the prisoner's.

'What if I have you whipped?'

The prisoner recoiled a pace.

'My Lord, I'm a pedlar, nothing more. I know nothing of what I carry. There are rich men in Pelidor....'

His voice quavered into silence as he realised none of the implacable faces watching him believed a word of what he said. He looked around him desperately, as if for a way of escape. Owain heard Richeldis take a deep breath as she stepped forward.

'My Lord, he may be telling the truth,' she said.

'Books from Centre still come to light. Probably this man cannot even read them.'

'And the cross?' Severan held it out so that she could see it clearly. 'Is he so woefully ignorant as not to know what that is?'

'But, my Lord—'

'Be quiet,' Arven interrupted. 'You're a foolish girl, you should attend to your stitchery and not meddle in what doesn't concern you. As for you—' He thrust his face close to the prisoner's again—'I will know what I wish to know, or your head will decorate my gates. Deal honestly, and you may have your freedom.' He paused as if he expected the prisoner to think better of his reply, but the man said nothing. Arven waved dismissively to the guards.

'Take him.'

He did not wait to see his order obeyed, but stalked off upstairs with Jerold at his heels. Richeldis was left facing Severan.

'My Lord—'

He silenced her with a quick gesture.

'Say nothing you might be sorry for. The man is guilty.'

He let the cross fall to the floor, and picked up the bag once again.

'You see, the books are new. They have come from a printing press on Centre, and recently at that. Can you expect Arven to do nothing? Now go—and forget this, for your own safety.'

He held her eyes steadily, and unwillingly she retreated to Owain's side.

'Go,' Severan repeated. Then his gaze went past

them to the door at their back. He seemed suddenly disconcerted. 'Hilarion—'

Owain swung round. Hilarion was standing by the door. His eyes, dark with pain, were fixed on his father, but as Severan spoke, he turned and left without a word. Severan took a pace towards the door, checked, and stood motionless. Owain saw Hilarion's pain reflected in his father's face, and realised again how alike they were. Then, seeming to realise he was watched, Severan stepped back and almost ran up the stairs. Owain felt shaken. He had never seen the man lose command of himself before.

A second later he had to put Severan out of his mind. Richeldis was tugging at his arm.

'Come on. I want to talk to you.'

Back in the passage there was no sign of Hilarion. He could have gone any one of several ways; he had not returned to their seat in the garden. Birds were pecking delightedly at the food they had left spread out. Richeldis shooed them away absently and sat down.

'Forget Hilarion for the moment. This man— we must do something.'

'What?'

'Get him away somehow. He must have friends here, and he'll betray them as soon as Arven starts to question him seriously. He knows he'll betray them, you could see it.'

She sank into deep thought. Owain selected bread and cheese from the napkin and bit into it. Being hungry, in his view, made it harder to think. He had to admit to himself that he could not possibly see what Richeldis could do—particularly when she might herself have to face Arven's questioning in a few days.

'You see what this means?' she asked after a few moments.

'Mmm?'

'Use your head, Owain. It means there must be people, here in Pelidor, who still serve the Lord. And they're in touch with Centre. Fern hasn't been abandoned after all!'

Briefly she was glowing, excited, but then the excitement died.

'They'll all be in danger if we can't do something. If we had money we could bribe a guard, perhaps.'

'Have you?'

'Nothing a guard would disobey Arven for. And not much to sell. Unless....'

She drew the wooden ball out of the pocket of her skirt where she always carried it.

'But you love it!' Owain protested. 'Your Lady gave it to you.'

'Yes, but it's not worth a man's life—several lives. Let it go.'

She tossed it to Owain, who, startled, just managed to catch it.

'Would you take it into the city for me? See what you can get for it. Sell it, if you think it would be enough.'

Owain had to agree; he knew it was stupid to feel reluctant.

'Now?' he asked.

'In an hour or so. The city will be busy then—you'll be less conspicuous.'

Her decision made, she turned to the remains of the food.

'And we must talk to Hilarion again,' she reminded Owain, as they finished their meal. 'I never had the chance to ask him about the ring, and I think he would have helped us.'

But when Owain went searching for Hilarion, the steward's son was, once again, nowhere to be found. Owain looked for him until it was time to go down into the city, and then gave up. Passing through the hall, on his way out, he remembered the cross the pedlar had been carrying. Severan had let it fall; Owain had a picture of it lying on the stone at the foot of the stairs. But the stone paving was now bare, and although Owain spent several minutes hunting around the hall, he did not find the cross.

9

Owain passed through the gate of the citadel, and instead of following the steep Street of the Councillors, turned right into a road which sloped more gently and led him at last into the busiest part of the city. At that hour, as Richeldis had expected, the streets were crowded. Shops were open, their merchandise displayed to the passers-by, traders were crying their wares, in a square beside a fountain a trio of acrobats were performing. Owain stayed to watch for a while, and then, remembering his errand, moved on, and began to look more closely for a shop where he might try to sell the carved wooden ball.

He had turned a corner down a narrow, quieter street when he saw ahead of him a familiar, black-clad figure and recognised Hilarion's limping walk. Pleased to have found him at least, he quickened his pace, wriggled between a pair of gossiping market women, ducked under the brightly coloured display of a linen weaver, and straightened up, to see nothing but the street empty in front of him.

He could see only one door that Hilarion could possibly have gone through. Without thinking, he followed. Hilarion's name died on his lips as he stepped into the shop and was overcome by a sudden pang of homesickness, sharp as a slap in the face. The room was dim after the bright sunlight in the street, so that it was a moment before his vision cleared and he realised he stood in a carpenter's shop. It was the smell he had noticed first, the tang of crisp wood planings littering the floor. The room was quite empty, but he thought he saw a slight movement in the curtain that covered the door at the back of the shop.

A moment later the curtain was pushed back and a man came in. He wore a carpenter's apron, but there the resemblance to Petroc ended. This man was slender, quick moving, with brown hair, brown skin and very dark eyes. Owain wondered if it was his imagination that he looked very slightly agitated.

'What can I do for you, lad?' he asked.

'I...I thought I saw a friend of mine come in here.'

The carpenter looked round the obviously empty shop.

'Lots of people come in here, lad,' he said brusquely.

By now Owain's curiosity was thoroughly aroused, but short of asking directly to look in the back room, there was nothing he could do to satisfy it. Instead, he pulled the ball out of his pocket.

'Would you be interested in buying this, master?' he asked.

The carpenter put out a hand and Owain handed the ball to him.

'Well now...a pretty toy.' He turned it over and over and parted the outer halves to reveal the first of the nesting balls inside. 'It's yours to sell?' he asked shrewdly.

Owain nodded. The carpenter seemed to believe him; at least, he relaxed and became more friendly.

'Fine workmanship,' he remarked. 'The work of a master.'

Owain basked in pride for the absent Petroc.

'Well now, lad,' the carpenter went on more briskly, 'I'd be interested in buying it, and I could sell it again, but I'd have to take thought for my profit. I'll give you five silver pieces for it, but I'm bound to tell you, you could get more if you sold it privately, maybe in the court. That's my advice.'

'Thank you.' Owain could not explain why it was impossible to sell the ball in the court. 'Thank you. I'll think about it.'

He left the shop, with an amiable farewell from the carpenter. He was thinking hard. Five silver pieces did not sound enough to bribe a guard; he would have to consult Richeldis. But that was not the only thing he had to think about. He was certain that Hilarion had entered the carpenter's shop, only a minute or two before his own arrival. He walked down the rest of the street; beyond the carpenter's shop, the other doors were barred, and the corner too far away for Hilarion, with his slow pace, to have reached in the time. Owain wondered if he should have questioned the carpenter further, but he was fairly sure, remembering the man's behaviour, that he would have got nowhere. And after all, it was none of his business.

The problem nagged at him, however, as he returned to the citadel. There were many reasons why Hilarion might have visited the shop, but no explanation, as far as Owain could see, of why he should hide. And why should the carpenter co-operate? Owain shrugged, trying to tell himself he had troubles enough of his own, but he could not forget the incident.

He tried to sell the ball in one or two other shops, but he had no better luck, and concluded that the carpenter had offered him a fair price. It was not going to be enough. Owain had never had much hope that they could do anything to free the pedlar, but he knew Richeldis would be disappointed.

He found her restlessly pacing her room.

'I tried to speak to Arven again,' she said, 'but he wouldn't listen. He just told me it was none of my business.' She was twisting her hands together as she spoke. 'And I've prayed—oh, I have prayed, Owain, but we must do something as well!'

Owain explained about the ball.

'Well, you did your best,' she said. 'If it isn't enough, it's not your fault. There must be another way.'

If there was another way, Owain could not see it. Hoping to distract her, he told her about his near encounter with Hilarion. She was inclined to be dismissive.

'Perhaps he wanted some work done.'

'But he wasn't in the shop at all. And why make such a mystery of it?'

'You're the one who's doing that.'

He could not get her interested, and she went back to worrying about the problem of the man from Centre. They spent the evening making and discarding plans, but in the end they had to give in, and when Owain left her to go to bed they were as far as ever from any solution.

As he closed the door of Richeldis' room behind him, Owain realised it was very late. A hush had fallen over the citadel. The torch at the turn of the tower stairs guttered in its holder. Owain found that he was creeping down the stairs and along the passage to his own tiny room, as if he had no right to be there, and was afraid of being discovered. A creaking sound from just ahead made him start, his heart racing.

He relaxed, annoyed with himself, when he saw a window shutter swinging open. If he went on like this, the mice of Pelidor would scare him to death! He went forward, meaning to fasten the shutter, and then paused in the window alcove, looking out into darkness. Below him was the city, but only one or two lights were showing, lonely in the night, and the sky was clouded, starless. Owain shivered. He was playing a game, he thought to himself. He would never belong here. If he felt uneasy as a servant, how would he ever become Pelidor's lord? Whatever Richeldis might say, he was never intended to rule.

He had been happy to think of himself as the son of Petroc the carpenter, but when that was taken away from him, his happiness had been replaced by the consuming need to find out who he really was.

Now that he had found it, it meant nothing. He could not feel that he was really Cador's son, the heir of Pelidor, the rightful lord. It was all wrong.

The window was big enough to climb through, and for a wild instant he was tempted to do exactly that; to escape, to return to the security of Petroc's house. Sighing, he closed the shutter and fastened it. He had rejected that temptation before. There was no going back. If he ran away, he would never find security again, only the taste of failure. He had to go on. But whatever lay ahead—death from Arven, or the lordship of Pelidor—he felt that Owain, his real self, whom he had thought he knew, would be lost for ever.

As he turned away from the window, another sound alerted him. But this one he could identify quickly—the uneven footsteps of Hilarion, and the tap of his cane. A second later, the steward's son appeared round the corner of the passage, and stopped dead.

'What are you doing here?'

Owain could have asked him the same question. It was too late for anyone to be about, except for guards on night duty. But Hilarion's expression did not invite anything that might be called impertinence. The thin features were cold, disdainful, the friendliness that he had begun to show completely wiped away.

'I have been attending my Lady,' Owain answered respectfully. 'She has only just dismissed me.'

Hilarion's dark eyes swept over him. For a moment it seemed as if he might question the truth of what Owain said. Owain realised that he ought to ask him about the falcon ring, or even to find out what he had been doing in the carpenter's shop, but in the face of this strange hostility, he found it impossible. Compromising, he said, 'My Lady was hoping to speak to you.'

Hilarion raised his brows, but said nothing.

'Perhaps you could attend her in the morning,' Owain suggested, feeling more awkward with every passing second.

'I shall try,' Hilarion replied. 'But I fear I might be otherwise occupied in the morning.'

He said this with an odd, challenging lift of the head, as if his words had another meaning, which he half-expected Owain to understand. Owain had no idea what it might be. He retreated a step or two.

'I'll tell her,' he stammered. 'And now...it's late—I....'

'You may go,' Hilarion said, impassively.

Owain was thankful to be released. As he glanced back, just before the next turn in the passage, he could see Hilarion still standing beside the window. In his stance and his expression there was a lonely defiance, as if he was prepared to stand alone against the whole world. Owain was tempted to go back to him. But he did not know what to do or say if he did, and after a second's hesitation he went on to his own room and his bed.

10

Owain was jerked into wakefulness by the beating of a great bell. Feet pounded past the door of his room. It was quite dark. Still bleary with sleep, he got out of bed, groped his way across the room and tugged the shutters open. Across the city, a pale line of light showed where dawn was breaking. The tumult outside his door was growing.

Hastily, Owain scrambled into his clothes. He was almost ready when there was an urgent knocking at his door. He opened it to let in Richeldis.

'What on earth is going on?' he asked.

She was alive with excitement.

'The prisoner!' she gasped out. 'The prisoner has escaped! Owain, did you do it?'

He shook his head. 'How could I do it?' he asked, bewildered. 'We couldn't think how—'

'Never mind,' Richeldis interrupted. She was pulling at his arm. 'Come on! I want to know what happened.'

She dragged him out into the passage, while he was still fastening the belt of his tunic. It was quieter now, and as they hurried along, the tolling of the bell suddenly stopped, leaving behind it a great silence.

'They're in the Hall of Council,' Richeldis explained. 'Arven will want to know what went wrong. I hope whoever did it has covered his tracks.'

They reached the doors of the hall as she finished speaking. They were double doors, standing wide open, but the entrance was blocked by a crowd of guards and servants who clustered there, trying to listen to what was going on inside. Owain could see and hear very little, no more than pillars and tapestried walls above the heads of the crowd, but by means of persistent wriggling, with an impatient

Richeldis behind him, he managed to squirm his way forward until he stood near the dais.

Arven was seated in a carved chair, with his son Jerold on one side of him, and Severan on the other. Owain noticed that while Arven and Jerold looked as dishevelled as he felt himself, Severan was fastidiously neat, as if being dragged out of bed at dawn was nothing unusual for him.

Two of the castle guards were standing at the foot of the steps to the dais, and one of them, an older man with grizzled hair, was speaking as Owain came up.

'...looked into the cell, my Lord,' he was saying. 'He was gone, but the door was still locked. They're sorcerers, they say, my Lord, some of these folk from Centre.'

'Rubbish!' Arven growled.

'Then how does a man get out of a locked cell, my Lord?'

Arven's hands were clenched on the arms of his chair. Owain could see that he was holding in furious anger.

'A man gets out of a locked cell when the cell is unlocked,' he stated, his self-control beginning to slip as he spoke. 'Because one of you is a traitor, and let him out. And I'll know which one before the day is much older!'

His last few words were rising to a shout.

'My Lord—' the guard was protesting.

A cool, incisive voice interrupted him.

'The guards know nothing, my Lord. I was responsible.'

There was a murmur of astonishment as the

crowd parted and Hilarion limped into the clear space before the dais. Arven half rose from his chair, and Owain saw Severan take a single pace forward.

'Explain yourself!' Arven ordered.

Hilarion gestured slightly towards the guards.

'Perhaps you had better hear their story, my Lord.'

The second guard, who had not yet spoken, cast a worried glance at him, and then addressed Arven.

'I was on duty, my Lord, when the prisoner was taken yesterday. Not long afterwards this lad came down and said he had orders to question him. I let him into the cell, and let him out again, about half an hour later. The prisoner was still there then.'

'I took over for the night duty.' The older guard continued the story. 'Hilarion here came to me and told me the same tale, and I let him into the cell. He wasn't there more than a few minutes, but when he came out he chatted to me for quite a while, telling me this and that about the prisoner, and what to do if he wanted to talk.'

'And where did this conversation take place?' Arven asked. He sounded quiet again, and all the more dangerous for that.

Hilarion's lips twisted into a bitter smile.

'We went to sit in the guard-room. I find it difficult to stand for very long.'

'And no one was outside the door of the cell?' Arven asked. The only response from Hilarion was a brief nod. Arven waved the two guards to one side, and they retreated, looking profoundly relieved.

'When you entered the cell for the second time,' Arven said softly, 'you took the prisoner a key, and with that key he released himself, while you were speaking to the guard. Now—' His voice suddenly became a bark. 'That key. Where did you get it?'

This time Hilarion did not respond at all, treating the question with an icy indifference. Owain watched, horrified and fascinated. He was beginning to understand something of what had been going on the night before; even the unfastened shutter fitted into the pattern. On the dais, Arven looked furious and baffled, Jerold was looking on with a kind of incredulous triumph, and Severan, white with shock, suddenly broke into speech.

'My Lord, if we might—'

Arven silenced him with a gesture. He bent forward towards Hilarion.

'I'm not a fool,' he said. 'There are two keys to those cells, one kept by the guard, the other I keep myself. You, apparently, used neither. It's clear you went somewhere, to some friends of that fellow, and they gave you a key—a master key—to release him. And where did you go? Not far. In the city, or maybe here in the citadel. Somewhere I'm harbouring a whole nest of spies and traitors, men from Centre, followers of their false god. And you know where they are.'

Hilarion had followed what he had to say attentively, but with a kind of cold detachment, as if none of it was anything to do with him.

'Well?' Arven asked.

'My Lord?'

Arven's head jerked back in anger.

'You know where they are,' he repeated. 'And I will know—now!'

Jerold grabbed at his father's arm.

'I could make him speak!'

Arven shook him off, but before he could say any more, Severan spoke again. His speech was hurried, urgent, with none of his usual delicate mockery.

'My Lord, if I might have some time alone with my son, I'm sure I could make him see reason. He's young, impetuous, he doesn't understand that—'

'I understand perfectly,' Hilarion interrupted.

Arven sat back with a sigh and looked up at his steward.

'I'm sorry, Severan,' he said. 'I understand how you feel, but it's gone beyond that now. This is plain treason.' He paused and then went on, 'You've served me well, and I don't want to cause you pain. I will give him twenty-four hours to come to his senses. After that....'

He shrugged. Severan bowed his head.

'You are generous, my Lord.' Arven snapped his fingers at the guards.

'Take him.' Then, as they started to move forward, he halted them with another gesture. 'No. No need for a cell. He's hardly likely to try...and he's your son, Severan. Go to your room, Hilarion, and stay there until you're sent for.'

Hilarion inclined his head slightly.

'My Lord.'

He was moving to withdraw when Jerold started forward, half sliding down the steps in his eagerness to confront him.

'He won't escape,' he said jeeringly, 'and without this, he can't even try.'

He tore the cane from Hilarion's grasp, and brought it crashing down on the edge of the dais. It splintered, and Jerold tossed the fragments contemptuously aside. With scarcely any change of expression, Hilarion turned and began, slowly and awkwardly, to make his way down the hall. Owain took a step towards him only to find that Richeldis was holding him back; he realised for the first time she had been gripping his arm painfully all the way through the interview.

'Later,' she breathed into his ear.

Arven suddenly got to his feet and raised his voice in a shout that echoed down the length of the hall, the release of pent-up frustration.

'Get out! All of you, get out!'

The crowds began to melt as if by magic, leaving the solitary, dark figure of Hilarion, still struggling towards the lower doors. Arven and Jerold left by a door at the back of the dais. Severan remained, staring down the hall at his son. Richeldis drew Owain back into the shelter of a pillar.

Suddenly, as the hall emptied, Severan moved forward.

'Hilarion!'

He left the dais and strode rapidly down the hall to where his son waited for him, a blankly courteous expression on his face. Severan stood over him, gripping his shoulders.

'Hilarion—please—tell me the truth, and I promise I'll save you. And I'll do my best to save those others, too.'

Hilarion looked up at him. Owain could not read his expression, but something there made Severan release him and step back. Without a word Hilarion turned and resumed his progress towards the doors. Stone-faced, Severan watched him out of sight.

II

Once again, night had fallen on Pelidor. Owain crept cautiously along the passage that led to Hilarion's room. Once he glanced back uncertainly to the corner, where Richeldis was keeping guard. She waved to him to go on. All day they had kept an unobtrusive watch. Severan had spent a long time with his son; Arven himself had paid a shorter visit. And in the intervals of watching, Owain and Richeldis had made a plan.

When Owain tapped on the door there was no reply. The handle yielded to his touch and he eased the door open. Inside the room it was dark, but the light from the passage showed him Hilarion, lying fully-dressed on his bed with his face turned to the wall.

'Hilarion!'

At the sound of his name, in Owain's urgent whisper, he turned and half sat up.

'Oh, it's you. What do you want?'

He did not sound friendly. Owain closed the door and stumbled forward in almost total darkness.

'Wait!'

Owain stood still at Hilarion's command, heard the scrape of flint and tinder, and then light sprang up from a taper at the bedside. When the twin flames were burning steadily, Hilarion looked up at him, a glint of flame reflected in the dark eyes.

'What do you want?' he repeated.

Owain crossed the room and sat, uninvited, on the end of the bed.

'I've come to help you,' he said.

'No one can help me now.' He sighed wearily and turned away. 'Leave me alone.'

'Richeldis and I, we've thought of what to do,' Owain went on, ignoring him. 'We're going to get you away.'

Hilarion looked up at him again. There was a faint trace of amusement in his voice.

'Don't be ridiculous.'

'It's not ridiculous.'

The familiar, bitter smile crossed Hilarion's face.

'Look at me! What possible chance could I

have? If they thought I could escape, they would have put me under guard.'

'But they didn't know you have friends to help you.'

Something in that struck Hilarion; he was silent, studying Owain intently. At last, frowning slightly, he shook his head.

'It isn't possible. I'm grateful, but I can't drag you into my danger. I knew what I was doing.'

Exasperated, Owain exclaimed, 'I think that's the last thing you knew!'

'What do you mean?'

Owain leaned forward, desperate for his attention. He had not come prepared to argue; he had expected to be on his way by this time. But knowing Hilarion, he reflected, he should have been prepared to argue.

'You set the pedlar free,' he said, 'but you put yourself in his place.'

'Not intentionally,' Hilarion assured him, with another flicker of amusement. 'If they hadn't discovered he was gone until after the citadel gates were opened, I could have walked out.'

'But they did,' Owain pointed out. 'You're still here, and you have secrets to betray now—such as what goes on in the carpenter's shop in the city.'

That was a wild shot, but it found its mark. Hilarion caught his breath.

'What do you know about the carpenter's shop?'

'I don't know anything,' Owain replied steadily. 'You followed me there.'

There was deep suspicion in Hilarion's voice,

and every scrap of colour had drained from his face until all that lived there were the wide, dark eyes.

'I heard you talking, through the curtain.'

'No,' Owain said, 'I didn't follow you, but I saw you there. I'm right, aren't I?'

Hilarion nodded.

'When I first spoke to the prisoner, he told me where to go. When you followed me into the shop, I thought perhaps Arven had sent you. And you were hanging about last night....'

Owain could not hold back his indignation.

'You thought I was a traitor!'

'There's no one I can trust, no one!' Hilarion retorted fiercely.

'Then listen,' Owain said. 'If I was serving Arven, he would know by now where you went. And we wouldn't be here now, going through this...stupid argument.'

Hilarion shook his head impatiently.

'Oh, I know that now.'

'As it is,' Owain went on, 'Arven doesn't know. But tomorrow morning he's going to start doing his best to find out.'

Hilarion sat up abruptly, eyes blazing. He had been coldly detached in the Hall of Council; now he was on fire.

'I'm not afraid, you know! I don't care what they do to me!' More quietly, he added, 'I was trapped here for years, forced into serving men I despised, and despising myself for not standing against them. I thought Centre had abandoned us. I even thought God had abandoned us. And now—you met the carpenter, didn't you? That's not all he is. He's a priest of the Lord, a man of Fern, but trained on Centre, and he's working here in secret—and there are others, here and there, all over Fern. Do you think it matters what they do to me, now that I know that?'

The outpouring had exhausted him, and he lay back against the pillows, staring up at Owain, who was more worried than ever. He reached out, daring to cover Hilarion's hand with his own.

'Are you sure?' he asked.

'I don't understand you.'

'Are you sure you can go on keeping silence, in spite of all that Arven can do to you?'

The slight frown appeared between Hilarion's brows again.

'Do you think I'm a coward?'

There was no anger in the question, only a faintly wondering tone, as if he too was considering the answer.

'I don't know,' he went on at last. 'Perhaps I am. I've never been tested like that. And tomorrow—' His voice broke on a sob. Terror swept into his voice like flood water breaking through a dam. 'I must keep silence! I've got to!'

Owain hated himself, though he was glad that Hilarion was at last waking up to reality.

'It will be all right if you come with us,' he promised.

Hilarion shook his head.

'I can't—I can't put you in danger.'

'You're not. Richeldis is already in danger, on her own account. I've been trying to persuade her to go, before it's too late. Now, with any luck, you can go together.'

'Richeldis.'

Hilarion repeated the name with a bewildered air, but it took only seconds for him to under stand.

'She knows something?' he asked, breathless. 'Something about the heir of Pelidor?'

'She does, and she was going to tell you about it when we were in the garden yesterday. Hilarion, it's not just for your sake that we want to get you out. We need your help.'

To his relief, that argument worked better than any of the others. Hilarion sat up, looking decided now, and ready for action.

'What do you want me to do?' he asked.

'Eat something first,' Owain replied.

He had already noticed the table with an untouched meal laid upon it, and guessed that Hilarion had never expected to need food again. Obediently Hilarion got up, and accepted support from Owain as far as the table. As he slid into a chair, he asked, 'What does she know?'

'I'd rather she told you that herself.' He grinned suddenly. 'You're going to get quite a surprise!'

He stood beside Hilarion, absent-mindedly chewing an apple while his friend made an attempt to eat something. But after a few minutes Hilarion pushed the tray away.

'I'm sorry, I can't. I'd rather go, Owain.'

'All right. Where's your cloak?'

'There, on the chest under the window.'

Owain was fetching it when a light tapping

came at the door. He stiffened, then blew out the taper. He heard the scraping of Hilarion's chair as he stood up. The door began to open. Then Owain stifled laughter as Richeldis' impatient whisper came through the crack.

'What's going on? Are you two going to sit gossiping here all night?'

12

Once he had made his decision, Hilarion was sensible enough, and he made no fuss about needing help. Leaning on Owain's arm instead of the cane, he progressed slowly along the passages, while Richeldis went swiftly ahead to make sure all was safe. She had already chosen a suitable window, not the one that the prisoner had escaped by on the previous night, but one closer to Hilarion's room, that gave onto the garden.

'There's a drop,' she explained in a whisper. 'Onto grass. No trouble at all.'

Owain went first, after they had listened for a few moments and heard nothing more alarming than an owl to break the stillness. The night was dark, with clouds covering the moon. Richeldis had not told him how far he would have to drop, but he held on to the sill, walked down the wall to the length of his arms, and then let go. He landed on springy turf no more than two feet below.

A moment or two later, Hilarion followed him, falling heavily. Owain helped him to his feet.

'All right?' he asked.

'Yes.' His voice was a little shaky, but steadied almost at once. 'I'm not used to leaving by this route.'

Owain's grin was unseen in the darkness, and his reply was prevented by the arrival of Richeldis, who landed neatly and looked around her.

'Nothing,' she murmured, satisfaction in her voice. 'And no one can see to follow us on a night like this.'

However, as they crept across the garden, and Owain's eyes grew used to the night, he realised it was not completely dark. A faint silvery glow behind the clouds showed where the moon was riding. A breeze was springing up; the clouds grew ragged. He guessed it would not be long before they would be torn away, and the brilliance of an almost full moon would light up their escape.

Leaving the garden would not be as easy as leaving the citadel itself. There was one gate, which of course was closed and guarded. The wall was low on the garden side, but it was a long way to the street below, too far to drop without risking injury. Owain could not see how Hilarion was going to manage it.

'We need a rope,' he muttered to Richeldis.

'A rope? You know we couldn't risk asking for

anything like that. Someone might have put two and two together.'

Owain relieved his feelings by taking a running jump at the wall, grasping the top and scrambling up, skinning his knees as he did so. Sitting astride, he looked down into the street. He was encouraged to see that the wall was not sheer, as he had pictured it; there were one or two projecting stones, one or two possible footholds. He thought he could manage it, and Richeldis, of course, could manage anything—but Hilarion?

Reaching down, he grasped Hilarion's hand, and helped him to drag himself up to sit on the wall beside him.

'What do you think?' he asked.

Hilarion shrugged. 'This was your idea.'

Owain gave him a look, but the clouds were really breaking up by now, and there was no time to waste in backchat.

'I'll go first and guide you down,' he said. 'Blame me if you break your neck.'

He edged his way along the wall to where a couple of projections gave them a good start, and swung himself over. Immediately he was conscious of the long drop to the street, and more than that, of how hazardous the whole thing must look to Hilarion. But his friend did not hesitate when ordered to follow. Owain forced himself to go slowly, examining all the possible handholds, aware that Hilarion's twisted foot was virtually useless, and choosing the route that looked easiest for him.

They had descended no more than a few feet

when the moon finally broke free of the clouds. Owain was almost dazzled. He could imagine what they must look like: two enormous black spiders, pinned to the wall by shafts of cold light. And at the same moment, he heard measured footsteps echoing up from the street below. Owain froze. He closed his eyes, praying fervently that Hilarion too would keep still.

He waited for the shout that would tell him they were discovered. It did not come. Gradually the footsteps died away.

'What was that?' he asked aloud.

He did not really expect an answer, but he heard Richeldis calling softly from above his head.

'A guard. I didn't know they patrolled.'

'We know now.'

'Owain.' That was Hilarion's voice, tightly controlled. 'I think I'm slipping. I can't—'

'Yes, you can.' Owain dragged his mind back to what he was supposed to be doing, and began issuing orders rapidly. 'Can you see that stone sticking out, about a foot to your left? Reach over. That's right. Fine. Now....'

It seemed like several years later that he realised he was far enough down to let himself drop into the street.

'I'm down,' he called up to Hilarion. 'You can let go.'

After a brief hesitation, Hilarion did as he was told. Owain steadied him as he landed.

'All right?'

He nodded. He was beyond speaking, shaking with the reaction of relief. But he had done it, and as he realised that, he smiled faintly. Owain patted his shoulder cheerfully, and turned to watch Richeldis coming down, all the while alert for the approach of another guard. Once she had joined them, they made for the comforting shadows of a street opposite, where they felt safe enough to rest for a while.

'Where are we going?' Hilarion asked.

'To see your friend the carpenter,' Richeldis replied promptly. 'After all, it's partly on his account that we're in this mess. He must have ways of hiding people. You in particular have got to disappear.'

Hilarion nodded thoughtfully. 'There must be something I could do to help, somewhere else.'

'There's something you can do to help here in Pelidor,' Richeldis told him, 'but this is hardly the place to talk about it.'

'Yes, Owain told me—' His voice quickened suddenly. 'He said you knew about the heir of Pelidor.'

'I do, but I'm not going to discuss it underneath this draughty wall. If you're ready, we'll go on.'

They went on, slowly now, but relaxing as they drew further away from the citadel. Hilarion was very tired, and leaning heavily on Owain, who realised that this was his second night without sleep. They were all glad when they rounded the corner that brought them to the door of the carpenter's shop.

The door was bathed in moonlight, but the house itself was dark and quiet. Owain left the other two in the shadows across the street, and went to knock at the door. There was no response. He knocked again, louder, and this time a head was thrust out from an upper window of the house next door.

'Who's that?'

'I was looking for the carpenter,' Owain called back.

'At this time of night?'

The head, or its owner, was obviously annoyed.

'An urgent message, Master,' Owain tried to explain.

'Comings and goings at all hours,' the head grumbled to itself, and then added to Owain, 'Well, he's not here. Can't you see he's not here? He went off first thing this morning, and I don't know when he's coming back. And you take yourself off, too, and let honest folk get a decent night's sleep. I don't know what the world's coming to.'

Still grumbling, the head retreated and the window was slammed shut. Owain gave one more look at the firmly closed door before he went to join Hilarion and Richeldis at the other side of the street. Above the huddled rooftops the moon rode serenely through the last tatters of cloud. They were free of the citadel, but they were trapped in Pelidor, and with the morning, the hunt would begin.

13

At the end of the next street they found a temporary refuge in the courtyard of an empty house. Hilarion, exhausted to the verge of collapse, slid almost at once into a troubled sleep, leaving Owain and Richeldis to plan their next move.

'I was relying on finding the carpenter,' Richeldis admitted. 'But I can understand why he isn't there. If he thought Hilarion was taken, he would have to disappear, to protect himself and the others.'

'So what can we do now?' Owain asked.

Richeldis was still following her own train of thought.

'If he is a priest of the Lord,' she said, 'I don't believe he would just abandon Hilarion. He must have left word with someone, in case Hilarion managed to reach him. But it's the middle of the night, so how can we find out?'

'If we wait until morning—'

'If we wait until morning,' Richeldis rejoined tartly, 'Arven will have roused the city and all three of us will be captured.'

'Then what?'

Richeldis leaned back against the courtyard wall.

'We need to get out,' she said. 'Out of the city, and find somewhere—in the forest, perhaps—where we can hide safely for a day or two. Then one of us can stay with Hilarion while the other comes back and tries to get in touch with the carpenter.' She sighed deeply, pushing back her hair. 'And that's easier said than done, too.'

Owain thought over the problem of leaving the walled city. The only possible way as far as he could see was through one of the gates, but by now the gate guards must know that Hilarion was a prisoner, even if they had not yet heard of his escape, and they would recognise him. By the way Richeldis was looking thoughtfully at their sleeping companion, he could see that she had her mind on the same difficulty.

'We might change clothes, or disguise ourselves somehow,' she murmured, 'but we couldn't disguise the way he walks. Going through the gates is just too risky.'

'I'm not going over any more walls!' Owain asserted.

Richeldis gave him a quick smile.

'No—but what about going under?'

At first Owain did not understand. 'If we had six months to dig a tunnel—'

'Don't be ridiculous. Haven't you noticed that there's a river, or a stream at least, flowing through the city? I could see it from my bedroom window. It must get out somewhere, and I don't see why we couldn't get out with it.'

To Owain, that sounded even more risky than walking through the gates.

'Where?' he asked.

'I don't know, but Hilarion might. I'll have to wake him.'

She leaned over and shook Hilarion's shoulder;

he roused slowly, bewildered for a moment and not knowing where he was. When Richeldis explained her idea to him, he nodded thoughtfully.

'I know where the stream comes in and out,' he said. He sat up, took a scrap of stone and sketched in the dust of the courtyard. 'There...and there. Here in the north, it's too close to the gate, but on the south side we might manage it, and that would bring us out near the edge of the forest. There's one problem, though.'

'There would be,' Owain said under his breath.

'There's an iron grating, set in the culvert—in case an enemy tried to get in that way.'

Owain was discouraged, but Richeldis got to her feet.

'We'd better go and look. After all,' she added cryptically, 'it's years since anyone has ever thought of attacking Pelidor.'

Hilarion directed them to the south side of the city, keeping for most of the way to narrow, winding back streets. They met no one. The stream, shallow enough to wade across, flowed through a stretch of open ground between the last of the houses and the wall.

'We stable the horses for the citadel down here,' Hilarion explained. 'There's water, and space to exercise them.'

He showed them where the stream disappeared into the culvert, a semi-circular black hole in the city wall. Owain did not like the look of it at all. As they drew closer, Richeldis knelt on the bank and tried to peer into the blackness.

'I can't see a thing,' she complained, 'but it

can't be very far. It's only the thickness of the walls.'

Owain looked at her and grinned resignedly.

'All right,' he said. 'I'll go and look.'

He lowered himself carefully into the water. It flowed deeper and swifter where it disappeared under the wall, but when his feet touched bottom he was submerged only to his waist.

'It's freezing cold,' he muttered to himself.

Steadying himself against the wall, he moved off downstream. He had to stoop; there was only about a foot of clear space between the roof and the surface of the water, but the air, encouragingly, was fresh. Soon he came to something that stopped him from moving on, and discovered, by touch, the grating Hilarion had spoken of. He half turned and called back softly to Richeldis, his voice echoing in the confined space.

'Well?' her voice came drifting down to him.

'I've found the grating.'

'Is it firm?'

He wrenched at the network of iron and found to his relief that it moved. A few more vigorous tugs almost brought it free, but there was one bar that resisted him. He felt that if he could only loosen it, the whole grating might swing back and let them pass. He got out his belt knife and began to chip at the stone where it met the bar, but he was working underwater, in pitch dark, and it was a slow business.

'What are you doing?' Richeldis' voice came again.

'Trying to shift this bar.'

There was silence for a few moments while Owain went on chipping, and then suddenly he heard the sound of movement in the water, and Richeldis spoke into his ear.

'Can you hurry up?'

He almost dropped the knife.

'What are you doing?' he asked, furious. 'I don't even know if I can get through.'

'There's someone up there,' she explained. 'A man with two buckets. It must be getting on for morning.'

'Did he see you?' Owain asked.

'No.'

'Then we'd better make sure we don't have to go back,' he said, attacking the stone once again. 'Is Hilarion all right?'

'Perfectly.' Hilarion's voice came back crisply. He almost sounded as if he was enjoying himself.

For the next few minutes there was silence. Owain realised that he could see the top bars of the grating, outlined faintly against a paler segment of a circle, the other end of the culvert. How far away was dawn, he wondered. Then he heard, distant but clear, the sound of someone whistling. He stopped chipping, fearful that the noise he was making had already been heard. His shoulders ached from his cramped position, and his hands were growing numb from working under the icy water. The whistling grew fainter, died away, and Owain heard Richeldis let out her breath in a long sigh of relief.

'He's gone.'

This time, when Owain set to work again, he felt

something give way almost immediately. He thrust at the grating. With a deep scraping sound, it moved back, pivoting like a gate, and he was able to force his way through. A moment later he was hauling himself out of the stream on the far side of the wall, and turning to give a helping hand to Richeldis and Hilarion. They crouched on the grass, wet and shivering, but free.

'At least we're free for the moment,' Richeldis said, standing up to wring water out of her skirts. 'We'd better get out of sight before the sun comes up.'

In the grey light of early morning they could see the road along which she and Owain had travelled when they came to Pelidor. To Owain it already seemed several lifetimes ago. He had entered the city believing that he was Pelidor's heir. Now he was leaving it as a fugitive, further than ever from proving who he was. They had been forced to discard their plans to find the man with the falcon ring. And as he too got to his feet and prepared to set out, Owain admitted to himself that he was not altogether sorry.

They were making for the forest, using the road at first for speed, and to help Hilarion, but as the light grew, the risk increased of meeting early travellers on their way to Pelidor. After a while they clambered across the ditch at the side of the road, down the bank and across the grassland to the edge of the trees. There was about half a mile of open country to cross before they could disappear. The sun was rising behind the trees, and deep shadows stretched towards them like arms welcoming them to safety. The city was falling away behind them, though they could hear faintly the sound of a trumpet on the walls, and fainter still the noise of early huntsmen calling their hounds together.

Owain was supporting Hilarion, who was exhausted but refusing to give in, seeming almost exhilarated by the success of their escape. The nearest trees were now only yards away. As they moved beneath the outermost branches, Richeldis turned. The wind brought the cry of the hounds floating down towards them. Owain halted, listening, and Richeldis whirled to face him, fear in her eyes.

'Owain—they're hunting us!'

14

Richeldis' fear was only momentary. Recovering, she moved rapidly to Hilarion's other side, and took his arm.

'Come on—quickly.'

'You can't be sure,' Owain objected, as she urged them deeper into the forest. 'They can't be hunting us. They would have lost the scent when we went into the culvert.'

'And they could pick it up again at the other

end. Don't argue, Owain. We have to move fast. It's our only chance.'

For the next few minutes they plunged through the trees, the crash of their own movements drowning any noise from their pursuers. Soon the going became more difficult, through thickets of bramble and fern that caught and tore at their clothes and hid the bumps and hollows in the ground.

For all the help they could give him, Hilarion was almost at the end of his endurance. Several times he would have fallen without Owain's arm to support him. Owain could hear his sobbing breath as he forced himself on, knew how much each stumbling step was costing him, and knew it would be useless in the end. Glancing back, he could see nothing, but he thought he could hear, still distant but growing closer, the clamour of the hunt. Then the ground gave way under his feet and he fell.

It was a soft fall onto bracken, and he was on his feet in a minute, holding out a hand to Hilarion who had fallen with him. His friend lay back against the slope and did not move, except to shake his head.

'I'm sorry. I can't. You go on. They won't follow you once they find me.'

'No.' That was Richeldis, sliding down the slope towards them, her face set and obstinate. 'We go together.'

Before he could protest she gestured him abruptly to silence.

'Listen!'

Now they themselves were still, Owain could hear clearly the steady baying of the hounds.

'Closer,' he muttered.

'Not that!' Richeldis was impatient. 'Down there—water. There must be a river. We can break the scent.'

Now that she pointed it out, Owain could hear running water, and noticed that the ground was softer and damp. Ignoring another protest from Hilarion, he pulled him to his feet and half carried him down the slope until they came in sight of the river.

It was fiercer than the stream they had already passed through, wider and deeper, running dark beneath the trees. They grew to the very edge, and thrust out gnarled roots into the water. Richeldis ran ahead, and then beckoned the others urgently. She pointed to a place where the water had undercut the bank, scouring out a hole for itself, and under the overhang they might, perhaps, remain hidden for a while.

'Down there!' she gasped. 'You go first, Owain. Take your cloak off—go on, quickly!'

Owain lowered himself into water that swirled round his shoulders. The cold took his breath away. Grabbing a projecting root, he braced himself against the bank. Suddenly he felt safe. No one would ever see him from above. He reached out to help Hilarion down and to guide him into the same refuge. He expected Richeldis to follow, but instead she bundled up the cloaks they had discarded and stood looking down at them.

'What are you doing?' Owain asked.

'Laying a false trail,' she replied.

Before Owain could do anything to stop her, she raised a hand and was gone, the sound of her swift footsteps lost almost at once in the increasing noise of the hunt. Hilarion made a sudden movement as if he would try to haul himself out and go after her, but Owain clutched at him and dragged him back.

'Keep still,' he hissed. 'We couldn't catch her. She can look after herself.'

He doubted it, in these circumstances, but he felt he had to reassure Hilarion. His friend's face was white with shock and exhaustion. Owain drew him in beneath the bank, trying to shield him from the main force of the water, and wondered how long either of them could be expected to go on.

The hunt was very close now. Owain could hear men crashing about in the undergrowth, shouting to each other above the noise of the hounds. The confident baying as they held to their scent had given way now to whining and snuffling, and Owain could picture them as they quested up and down the bank above his head. Overhanging grasses hid him and blocked his view; he could catch a glimpse of the opposite bank, but nothing of what was going on a foot or so above his head.

He lost count of how long he stood there, with water lapping round him, one hand grasping the root and the other arm round Hilarion's waist. Gradually he began to make out two voices and guessed that their owners were slowly approaching along the bank. As they drew near, he recognised one of them: Jerold.

'...dogs worse than useless if they can't follow a

plain scent. Something must have happened here!' He sounded angry and frustrated. 'Or did they cross the river, do you think?'

By the time he finished speaking, Owain thought that he must be standing on the bank directly above his head.

'Perhaps, my Lord,' a second voice replied. 'But I doubt it.'

He recognised that voice, too; the cool, clipped tones of Severan. He glanced at Hilarion, and just in time tightened the grip he had on him, as his hands slid from the root he was clinging to, his eyes closed, and his body sagged as if he was slipping into unconsciousness.

'No!'

He tried to put all the force he had left into that one word, in a desperate undertone that, to his relief, reached Hilarion; a hand groped for the root and held on again, his eyes flickered open, but he scarcely seemed to breathe as he listened to his father's measured tones from the bank above him.

'My son will undoubtedly be too exhausted to swim the river. We must go on searching on this side. They can't be far away.'

'There!'

Jerold's voice changed suddenly to eager anticipation, and for a dreadful second Owain thought they had been seen. Then he realised that the hounds had struck a new scent, and were moving off again downstream, following Richeldis. His fears for her increased as the sounds of the hunt moved away. At last he could hear nothing but the quiet rush of the water, broken only by a very distant shout or the cry of a hound. He realised that for the moment the hunt had passed them by.

He shook Hilarion, who still stood transfixed, gazing upwards.

'Are you all right?' he asked. 'Don't frighten me like that again, please.'

'He was there,' Hilarion breathed out. 'Hunting us. I didn't think...even he—'

His voice sounded unutterably desolate. Owain could not bear the pain of it.

'Come on,' he said briskly. 'Let's get out of this. You need to rest.'

Hilarion turned his head, really looking at him at last.

'Do you think we should cross?' he asked. 'You heard what...what he said. They'll search on this bank, not the other.'

Owain parted the grasses and looked across the river. He could see little, but there was good cover on the other side, whatever else there was.

'Can you manage it?' he asked.

Hilarion's only reply was a nod, but he was looking as obstinate as Richeldis at her worst. He waited only for a word of agreement from Owain before striking out into the current. Owain followed.

He guessed that at his best Hilarion was a strong swimmer, but he was desperately tired now, and weighed down by heavy, waterlogged clothing. He kept going, and Owain kept pace with him; there was a moment when he thought he would need help, but it passed, and the opposite bank drew closer. They were being carried downstream, following their pursuers, but Owain saw nothing of them.

Soon they approached a clearing where the river grew wider and shallower. Owain felt the bottom, managed to stand, and saw that Hilarion too had found his feet. He went to help him as he struggled towards the bank, but before he reached him Hilarion stumbled and fell, pitching forward on his face, half in and half out of the water. He made no effort to get up.

Owain knelt beside him. One look at him was enough to make him realise that this time, at last, he had come to the end. His eyes were half closed, his breathing harsh and shallow. Owain put an arm round his shoulders.

'Hilarion, please,' he urged gently. 'Just a little further. We must get under cover.'

Hilarion heard him. His eyelids fluttered and he tried, ineffectually, to raise himself. Owain slid an arm under him, lifted him, and dragged him a few yards up the bank, until they could both collapse in the shelter of the great arching clumps of bracken that covered the slope. It was all he could do. He lay beside Hilarion, shivering, listening, with no idea at all what his next move could be.

15

After a while, Owain recovered enough to begin wondering about Richeldis. Listening carefully, he could hear nothing but the ordinary sounds of the forest. He knelt and peered over the tops of the bracken. There was no sign of movement in any direction. Even when he dared to stand, he could still see nothing. He wanted to set off downstream and look for her, but he knew he had to stay with Hilarion.

His friend was lying inert, his eyes closed, but Owain did not think he was sleeping naturally. His breathing was still fast and harsh. For the first time Owain began to worry; although they had escaped, for the present at least, they had no food or money or proper shelter, and he guessed that Hilarion would be ill if he was not cared for.

While he was thinking, he peeled off his sodden tunic, wrung out the water from it, and for want of anything better, put it back on again. He was just fastening the belt when he heard light footfalls approaching, and a voice softly calling his name.

Owain sprang to his feet.

'Richeldis!' he exclaimed thankfully.

'That's right. Tell the whole of Pelidor we're here.' Her voice was irritated, but then she smiled. 'Thank goodness I've found you. Where's Hilarion?'

'Here.'

He pointed down into the bracken, and

Richeldis came up the slope to join them. Owain thought she was looking unreasonably neat and tidy, and dry, except for her feet and the draggled hem of her skirt. She carried their cloaks rolled up under her arm.

'What happened to you?' he asked.

At first she did not reply as she knelt beside Hilarion. Her face was troubled. At once she started to strip off his wet clothes, and as Owain helped her, she gave him a rapid account of what she had been doing.

'I followed the river for a while, and then, once it was shallow enough, I waded along by the bank to break the scent. Then I climbed a tree and watched them looking for me.' She gave a satisfied smile. 'You're quite right, Owain, no one ever looks up. When they were out of sight I thought it would be safer if I could cross, so I did.'

'What did you do, fly?'

'There was a fallen tree. Here, help me with this.'

Owain raised Hilarion while Richeldis eased his cloak around him. The movement, or the warmth, roused him and he opened his eyes, but it was hard to tell whether he recognised either of them, and he turned his head away.

'Hilarion, don't give up now!' Richeldis begged.

'His father was there,' Owain explained, and told her briefly of what they had heard under the river bank. 'He had to swim the river because Severan said he couldn't,' he concluded, 'but that was all he could do. I don't think he cares any more.'

'Well, he's got to care,' Richeldis said stubbornly. 'We've got to find better shelter than this, while we decide what to do.'

Again she bent over Hilarion and shook him, not too gently. He roused, and this time tried to sit up. Owain got an arm round him, and together they pulled him to his feet.

'We won't get far,' Owain said.

'We won't have to,' Richeldis assured him. 'I know a place, beside that fallen tree. It's only just round the next bend.'

Very slowly now, and exposed to anyone who might be searching for them, they made their way along the river bank. When they drew near to the fallen tree, Owain could see that it had pulled down part of the slope with it as it fell, and behind the roots, which writhed up well above his head, there was an open space, not big enough to be called a cave, but a good enough refuge for the time being.

They crept inside. Owain remained near the opening, to keep watch, while Richeldis drew Hilarion further in and lowered him to the ground with his back against the earth wall.

'I'm sorry,' he said. 'It was hearing him—my father....'

'I know,' Richeldis said softly. 'You don't hate him at all, really, do you?'

He shook his head, trying to speak, but instead he gave way to silent, anguished weeping. Richeldis exchanged a glance with Owain, full of compassion, and then comforted Hilarion until the fit was spent.

'You've got us now,' she said, when it seemed as if he might be listening. 'We won't leave you, and whatever happens, we'll face it together.'

Hilarion looked up at her.

'I used to love him and admire him,' he whispered, 'more than anyone I've ever known. But I've had to learn that nothing means more to him than his loyalty to Arven. I've seen him turn away from the real good of Pelidor, and even from his faith in God, but I suppose I've always hoped that there would be something—something he wouldn't betray. I suppose I thought he wouldn't betray me, but he was there, hunting us down.' He shuddered convulsively, and then was still. 'I'm sorry. It's over now.'

Richeldis reached out and took his hand.

'I never knew my father,' she said. 'But my Lady used to tell me that God is my father. He's yours, too, Hilarion. And he never betrays any of us.'

Hilarion nodded, silent. To Owain it seemed as if Richeldis had lifted him out of his pain, at least enough for him to face it and fight with it. Perhaps she felt the same, for when she spoke again it was in a very different tone, severely practical once again.

'And now we have to decide what to do.'

Owain could not help feeling that their position was almost hopeless, but he would not have dreamed of interrupting.

'We need food, more than anything,' Richeldis went on. 'And a place where we can really rest, and eventually we have to get away from here. I think the carpenter would help us, if we could find him, but to do that, one of us at least would have to go back into Pelidor.'

'I'll go,' Owain offered at once, and then added, 'Not that I like the idea.'

Richeldis gave him a crooked smile.

'Going back into Pelidor is the last thing they would expect us to do. The trouble is, we can't be sure that the carpenter left any message behind him. In any case, I don't think that's our first problem. Food and shelter are.'

She was silent for a while, considering. Owain sat in the sun at the mouth of their cave, also trying to think, but feeling how easy it would be to fall asleep.

'If we went to a farm we could work for some food,' Richeldis continued, 'and perhaps they would let us sleep in a barn. Or there's this.' She drew out the carved wooden ball again. 'We could still sell it, if anyone would buy it.'

'We would need to go back into Pelidor to do that,' Owain said.

'True. What was the carpenter going to give you for it—five silver pieces? That would buy us food, but it wouldn't get us very far along the road, if we have to go alone.'

'No, but this might.' Hilarion suddenly entered the conversation, pulling off a ring as he spoke. 'It might fetch the price of a horse, or a pack pony, at least. I should get along all right if I could ride. Owain, if you are going back into Pelidor, you could take it and sell it.'

He reached out and handed the ring to Owain, who took it, listening to what he had to say, and glanced at it casually. Then he froze. For a few seconds he forgot about breathing. Hilarion's voice seemed to come from a great distance. It was only when he heard Richeldis asking sharply, 'What is it?' that he pulled himself back to reality. Wordlessly, he held out the ring, and Richeldis looked at it. It was a heavy, silver ring, and the dark stone was incised with the device of a falcon's head.

16

'Hilarion, where did you get this?' Richeldis asked.

Hilarion looked bewildered, but he replied quite readily.

'It was my father's.'

'And where did he get it?'

'Why—from his father. It's always worn by the eldest son of our house.'

Richeldis turned triumphantly to Owain.

'Then it must have been Severan we were looking for all along! Of course, he fits your description perfectly, but he didn't wear the ring, and so we didn't think—'

'What do you mean?' Hilarion interrupted. 'Why is the ring important?'

Richeldis exchanged a glance with Owain, and

he gestured to her to tell Hilarion the story. He did not feel capable of it. Instead, he listened, turning the ring in his fingers, while Richeldis unfolded all they knew about the visit to Petroc, and about Owain's true identity as the heir of Pelidor.

'But that's impossible!' Hilarion protested as she finished.

Owain felt a wave of embarrassment washing over him. 'I know I'm not—' he was beginning.

Hilarion interrupted impatiently. 'I don't mean that. I mean, if it was Severan—' Owain noticed that he did not say 'my father'—'if it was Severan who took you there, why is he helping Arven to look for you? He thinks he knows where you are. He could have sent men to Petroc to have you arrested and brought to Pelidor, or killed in secret.' He looked straight at Owain. 'Why are you still alive?'

'We know that someone went to Petroc from Lady Isolda,' Richeldis pointed out. 'The carved ball proves that. Petroc made it.'

'Are you sure?' Hilarion asked.

Owain nodded. 'I would know his work anywhere.'

'And why would Lady Isolda entrust her child to Severan?'

Hilarion's voice was shaking with disgust. Richeldis quietly covered his hand with her own.

'I thought that too, at first,' she said. 'But he was a faithful servant to Lord Cador. Arven had only just come to power when the child was born. My Lady had no reason not to trust Severan then.'

'But she must have realised,' Owain broke in.

'When Severan chose to follow Arven, I mean. She must have realised what a mistake she'd made.'

Richeldis shook her head. 'I don't know. I was only a baby myself. And when I was older, she never spoke much about these things. She seemed...confident, though. As if she was waiting. I suppose she thought that as long as she knew where the child was—'

'Assuming Severan told her the truth about where he took him—me, I mean.'

Richeldis stared at him. That had obviously never occurred to her.

'And why didn't he kill the child outright?' Hilarion added harshly.

Richeldis tightened her grip on his hand.

'Hilarion, he's not a monster. All right, he knew, or thought he knew, that he had to turn and serve the new power in Pelidor. But that doesn't mean that he would willingly murder a baby. Do you really think that he would?'

Hilarion hesitated for a moment and then shook his head.

'But then, why is he looking for me?' Owain asked.

'Pretending to look,' Richeldis corrected him. 'Listen, I think I can understand how it was. He wouldn't tell Arven what he knew. Of course, he would pretend to search for you, but all the while he would know that you were growing up, the son of Petroc the carpenter, with no idea at all of who your true parents were, and you would never come to claim Pelidor. Eventually, because there wasn't anyone else, the Lords Councillors would have to confirm Arven as Lord. Severan gets what he wants, and doesn't have a murder on his conscience. I call that clever.'

Owain murmured agreement.

'The only thing it doesn't take into account,' Richeldis went on thoughtfully, 'is what he thought he was going to do if Lady Isolda was still alive when you came of age. If he lied to her, he couldn't go on lying then.'

'Don't ask me,' Owain said. His head was whirling at the thought of Severan's double dealing, and while he could not imagine how the steward had intended his plots to work out, he was sure that there would be some neat twist to his scheme, ready to be put into operation. He shivered. He did not like the thought of being pitted against a man like that. He wondered whether he could draw Severan over to his side, whether having turned traitor once, the steward would turn again and support the true heir. What would happen if he went to Severan and told him who he really was?

He rejected the idea almost at once, not daring even to suggest it to Richeldis. The risk was too great. Severan had made his decision, sixteen years ago. He served Arven, and he had disposed of Owain too cleverly to want him reappearing now. If Severan had had his way, Owain could have lived out his life quite contentedly as the son of Petroc the carpenter, apprentice, and eventually a master craftsman in his own right, without ever dreaming that he had the right to lordship. A twinge of regret went through him. Quite a large part of him would have been perfectly happy to have fallen in with Severan's wishes.

'And what about the ring?'

Richeldis' voice broke into his musings. Owain glanced down at the ring he still held.

'Not that one. The other—the ring of Pelidor.' She paused and then went on, 'Severan has it, of course.'

'Why?'

'Lady Isolda said she gave the ring to the heir. Of course, she didn't, not exactly, not when you were a tiny baby. She gave it to Severan. And Severan kept it. He wouldn't hand over the ring of Pelidor to a mere carpenter. And he wouldn't dare to get rid of it.'

Her explanation seemed to satisfy her, but Owain was still confused.

'So he pretends to search for the ring as well. But Arven needs the ring, if he's to be confirmed as Lord.'

'No he doesn't. He would like it, because that would mean that no serious claimant could ever come to unseat him, but he doesn't need it. The Lords Councillors will have to accept him in the end. All Severan has to do is hide the ring, keep his mouth shut, and wait.'

'So why doesn't he tell Arven?'

Richeldis laughed.

'Can you imagine Arven waiting for anything if he could do it another way?'

She turned to Hilarion.

'Have you ever seen the ring? It's gold, with a ruby. Have you ever seen your father with it?'

Hilarion shook his head slowly. 'I'm sure it's not in our rooms at the court. There's nowhere there to hide anything. I don't see....' His voice trailed off, and then grew excited as he added, 'I know where it could be!'

'Where?'

'In our old house in the Street of the Councillors. It's been shut up ever since we left. Some of our things are still there. And I—' He caught his breath. 'I've got a key!'

He put his hand to where his belt would have been if Richeldis had not taken off his wet clothes. She pointed wordlessly to the sodden bundle she had dumped on the floor of the cave. Hilarion scrabbled at it and came up with a leather pouch which he tipped out, spilling a coin or two, a seal and wax, and a long, thin key with intricate wards. Richeldis picked it up.

'Now,' she said, 'we have to go back into Pelidor.'

17

After more discussion they decided that they must re-enter Pelidor towards evening, buy what food they could with the little money they had between them, and go to search the house in the Street of the Councillors after dark. It would make the search more difficult, but the risk of being seen during the day was too great.

By this time it was about mid-day.

'We can afford some time to rest,' Richeldis said. 'Though one of us ought to keep watch. Not you,' she added to Hilarion. 'You've been through quite enough already. Get what sleep you can. Owain, I'll take first watch, you're falling asleep as well.'

Owain denied it, not entirely truthfully, but he would never have dreamed of disobeying her. He wrapped his cloak around himself and prepared for sleep. Hilarion was doing the same, but before he settled down, he said awkwardly to Owain, 'When you are Lord in Pelidor...my father—you won't...'

'No, of course not.'

Even while he reassured Hilarion, Owain felt his breath taken away by the speed with which a man's life had been placed in his hands. Was that what it meant to be Lord in Pelidor? If it was, it was more frightening than he had ever thought possible. He pushed the unwelcome ideas away and went to sleep.

It seemed only moments later that Richeldis roused him, but the shadows told him it must be mid-afternoon.

'I can't keep awake any longer,' she confessed. 'Everything's quiet. I don't suppose there'll be any more trouble until we try to get back into Pelidor.'

With this encouraging observation she lay down and rolled herself in her cloak.

'Wake me towards sunset,' she said, and closed her eyes.

Owain blinked himself awake and looked around. Hilarion was still asleep. Richeldis had wrung out his wet robe and hung it to dry on the tree roots. As she had said, everything was very quiet, except for the usual sounds of the river, the wind in the trees, and woodland creatures going about their business. Leaning back against the bank, Owain felt it would be very easy to doze off again.

Warily he unfolded cramped limbs and ventured out of the shelter to look up and down river. He could still see nothing; the hunt had drawn off for the time being. He passed some time by trying to think of a foolproof plan for getting safely back into Pelidor, but soon he abandoned the attempt.

Instead, he took his belt knife, cut a strong ash sapling, and began to trim it into a staff for Hilarion. Even a simple task like that, the feel of the wood and the memory of his old skills, was soothing, and for a while he managed to forget that he was the heir of Pelidor, with enemies who would take his life.

He roused his friends in the late afternoon. The gates of Pelidor closed an hour after sunset, which gave them plenty of time, even allowing for caution and Hilarion's infirmity. They were all three refreshed by sleep, though now Owain felt sick with hunger, and guessed that the others were no better. It was not even the time of year to find nuts and berries in the forest.

The first obstacle was the river, which they

crossed by the fallen tree. Owain and Richeldis found this easy, and Hilarion showed a grim determination that soon overcame his difficulties. Once he was on the opposite bank, with the staff that Owain had made for him, he was able to get along without much trouble.

Following the river bank, they soon arrived at the spot where Owain and Hilarion had hidden in the early morning. The grass and undergrowth were trampled down, and there was still a clear trail leading back in the direction that they and their pursuers had come. Cautiously they followed it.

The sun was going down ahead of them when they reached the edge of the forest. Pelidor was a black outline against the blazing sky. Coming from the shade of the forest, their eyes were dazzled, and they had taken several steps into the open before they were alerted to danger, and then it was sound, not sight, that warned them: a distant horn call, off to the right, towards the road, answered at once by another to the left, along the line of the trees. Owain grabbed Hilarion and dived with him into the cover of the bracken at the edge of the forest. Richeldis followed.

'They're watching!' Owain gasped.

'We should have known,' Richeldis said in a furious whisper. Owain realised she was angry with herself. 'They had us penned in there. All they had to do was wait for us to come out.'

As she spoke she began worming her way backwards into deeper cover. Owain saw that Hilarion was following, and then he himself began to crawl in the opposite direction, back towards the open grassland. He ignored Richeldis' low-voiced but irate calling of his name.

If I'm Lord of Pelidor, he thought, it's time I started proving it.

Wild ideas went through his head of walking out and giving himself up. If he announced who he really was, could he buy his friends' lives with his own?

No, he reflected ruefully. No one would believe a word of it.

Reaching the edge of the trees, he peered out. As his eyes grew used to the stronger light, he could see horsemen wheeling across the meadow, and a larger group moving down purposefully from the direction of the road. They were converging on a spot close to where he was hiding, but beyond them, to the left, everything seemed quiet. Owain wondered if they might work their way along under cover of the trees, and try to emerge some way to the south. But what would be the good of that? They might avoid immediate capture, but there would be no hope of reaching the gates of Pelidor. He began to feel desperate. Another night in the open, without food, would probably leave them fit for nothing but surrender.

A rustling in the undergrowth announced Richeldis, wriggling her way towards him and looking thoroughly annoyed.

'What do you think you're doing?'

'Looking. Richeldis, suppose I dashed out and drew them off? You might be able to get away, with Hilarion, and—'

'Don't you dare do anything so stupid!' she hissed at him. 'You would get a spear in the back before you'd gone ten yards. They're armed, or hadn't you noticed?'

Owain had noticed, but was hoping she had not.

'What then?' he asked.

'Hilarion has an idea. He says that if we go south from here, we soon come to the stream that flows through Pelidor. And if we follow that, we come to some old mine workings. We might be able to hide there.'

'Don't we have to cross the river again?'

'No, he says the river curves away. We have to cross the stream, but we can wade that.'

Owain could think of nothing better, and by now the two groups of horsemen had met, and were advancing towards their hiding place. As silently as they could, they made their way back to Hilarion, and struck off to the south. Owain was wretchedly conscious that it was exactly the opposite direction from the one they really wanted. Behind them, it sounded as if some of the horsemen had dismounted and were hacking at the undergrowth with swords, but gradually the sound died away behind them. When all was quiet again, Richeldis judged that they could afford to rest.

'We'll have to try again tomorrow,' she sighed. 'Really, if God wants his priests restored to Pelidor, he might make it a bit easier for us!'

They allowed themselves no more than ten minutes' rest. Already they could hear the gurgle of water ahead, and soon after setting off again they reached the stream. By now the sun had gone down. Owain welcomed the approaching darkness if it would hide them from their enemies, until he remembered that it would also hide their enemies from them.

They waded across the stream just inside the forest, but after that, if they wanted to reach the mine workings, they had to leave the shelter of the trees. Owain felt apprehensive, remembering what had happened last time. But for the first few hundred yards, all was quiet. Then chaos was unleashed.

In the twilight Owain was not sure what was happening. The first thing he saw was that the greyness ahead of him was thickening strangely and growing more intense, until within a few seconds a shape like a doorway, pulsing grey shot with silver, had formed across their path. He halted, blinking as if it was a vision arising from his own weariness. But Richeldis' arm gripping his, and Hilarion's sharp intake of breath, told him they had seen it too. And out of it, where seconds before there had been nothing, stepped a man. Owain could not make out his features, but something about him looked familiar.

He paused, glancing around him. Then he saw the three fugitives on the path and stepped forward, with an exclamation that was drowned by a sudden drumming of hoofbeats as a group of horsemen swept across the ridge and down towards the stream. The strange man's exclamation became a shout. He was beckoning. Owain looked at Richeldis. Their enemies were less than a minute away; the only alternative was that doorway. The man shouted again. He was running towards them. Suddenly, Richeldis moved, thrusting Owain forward.

'Go on!'

'But we can't—'

The man was beside them now, grasping Hilarion's arm as if he knew that he needed help. Somehow, Owain was running now, towards that shining shape. He expected it to burn him, consume him, but as he passed through it he felt nothing but a slight tingle. The splash and clatter of horsemen crossing the stream was cut off abruptly, and Owain realised that the rough surface of the path had become smooth. He was standing on polished metal. He was in a passage whose walls and roof were metal. At the end stood two men in grey uniform.

Owain whipped round, just in time to see the pulsing grey curtain fade and become a wall indistinguishable from the others. In front of it stood Richeldis and Hilarion, almost clinging together, and beside them, the man who had brought them there. In a better light, Owain recognised him at once. He was the priest-carpenter from Pelidor.

18

'We're *where?*' Richeldis asked, her voice expressing utter incredulity.

The carpenter grinned; he was obviously enjoying himself.

'You're on board a spaceship,' he repeated. 'In orbit around Fern. At present—oh, about twenty-five miles above Pelidor.'

One of the men in grey uniform strolled down the passage towards them. He had an air of authority about him, and Owain guessed he was one of the officers of the ship.

'Welcome aboard,' he said. 'Gildas, what's going on?'

'They were being hunted down,' the carpenter explained. He put a hand on Hilarion's shoulder. 'This is the boy I told you about.'

'Then you're even more welcome,' the officer said. 'Gildas, when you told me what he had done, I thought we'd heard the last of him. It took courage.'

'Oh, no...it wasn't—' Hilarion began, thoroughly disconcerted by the unaccustomed praise. His voice wavered and he put a hand to his head.

'He's worn out,' the officer said. 'They all are. Gildas, see to them, will you? We'll talk later.'

In the next hour, Owain saw so many incredible things that in the end he had no more room for amazement. He was taken to a room even smaller than the one he had occupied in Pelidor, where everything he might need—table, bed, cup-boards—were fitted into the walls. He bathed under a stinging shower of hot water in a tiny cubicle. When he came out, fresh clothes had been put out for him, and these at least were little different from what he might have worn at home, except that the fabric was richer.

When he was ready he emerged uncertainly into the ship's corridor to see Richeldis, also newly dressed, coming out of a similar door nearby. Gildas was waiting for them. He pressed a button and a section of the corridor wall slid back to reveal a small square space.

'The lift,' Gildas said, gesturing for them to go in.

To Owain that explained precisely nothing, but he obeyed, and at the touch of another button the door slid shut again. There was a slight jerk.

'We are now travelling,' Gildas said, 'perhaps as fast as a moderately fast horse—but only, of course, in relation to the ship. We're going to the observation deck.'

That again meant nothing to Owain until they stepped out of the lift a moment later, and he found himself confronting a vast sweep of window; beyond it was blackness, and the dazzle of a thousand stars. The magnificence of it took his breath away.

'When I come on board I always make for this,' Gildas said. 'You see nothing like it from Fern.'

When Owain could drag his eyes away, he saw that Hilarion was already there, curled up in a padded chair, and oblivious of their approach. His face as he gazed out was rapt with delight. Owain remembered his lonely frustration in the citadel garden, and the longing in his voice as he spoke of the ships. Perhaps all Hilarion had suffered would be worth it, in exchange for these moments of revelation.

He turned his head as Owain slid into the seat beside him, and let out a long sigh of contentment. He had nothing to say.

'I've asked them to bring us some food here.' Gildas' voice brought them down to earth, in one sense at least. 'I thought you might not feel like the ship's dining-room. And we ought to talk in private.' He looked down at Hilarion and ruffled his hair. 'I was afraid I wouldn't see you again,' he said. 'And I felt as if I was letting you down. I left a message for you with the linen-weaver up the street, but—'

'We came in the middle of the night,' Richeldis explained, as she took her seat. 'Did the pedlar get away?'

'Oh, yes. No trouble there. He's well away, and we won't put him at risk again. He shouldn't have been sent in the first place, it was asking too much of him, but the regular courier was ill.'

'The regular courier.' Richeldis repeated the phrase thoughtfully. 'You have an...an organisation, then?'

'You could call it that.'

'So Centre hasn't abandoned us!'

Gildas smiled at her.

'Not exactly. The rulers of Centre are a mixed lot. Some of them don't accept the Church, and of those who do, some just want to mind their own business. But there are some who care about what happens outside their own domains, and they're helping the Lord's work on Fern. When the priests were banished from Pelidor, and then from other places, some of us wanted to stay, and so we had to go underground. Our friends on Centre help us with money and books, and take anyone who wants to learn to be a priest. And so we go on. But it isn't easy—' his cheerful expression faded— 'and it's very little that we're able to do.'

'You might be able to do more before very long,' Richeldis told him.

Gildas' startled response was cut off by the arrival of some of the ship's crew with food. Even here, he seemed to think it was better not to talk until they were alone again. The meal that was set in front of them was simple, no different from the kind of food they might have been offered in Pelidor. Owain surprised himself by being more interested in the conversation. Though the soup, bread and cold meat were very welcome, he kept most of his attention for Gildas and Richeldis.

When they could talk freely again, she told Gildas the whole story, from her meeting with Owain on the road, leading up to their discovery that it was Severan who had taken Owain to Petroc, and who probably had the ring of Pelidor in his keeping. Most of the food was finished before she brought her account to an end. Gildas was frowning.

'So it's Severan you're up against,' he commented. 'A dangerous man, from what I've heard, and a clever one. Once he was a friend of the Church, but he turned away to serve Arven. So you're his son...'

He gave Hilarion a long, considering look, and Hilarion could not meet his eyes. Gildas turned the look onto Owain.

'And you're the heir of Pelidor. Well....'

'Once he is Lord,' Richeldis said, 'the priests can return to Pelidor.'

Gildas nodded.

'And how would you go about ruling in Pelidor,' he asked, 'when you were brought up in a carpenter's house?'

That question had been worrying Owain, but before he could reply, Richeldis responded tartly, 'Our Lord was brought up in a carpenter's house.'

Gildas glanced at her, half reproving. 'Let the boy answer for himself.'

'I don't know,' Owain answered honestly. 'But I would do my best—and I would have good advice.'

To his surprise, Gildas looked as if he was satisfied with the answer.

'So what do you want from me now?' he asked.

This time Richeldis left Owain to reply.

'We have to find the ring,' he said slowly. 'And for that, we have to get into Severan's old house. Can this ship put us down inside Pelidor?'

Gildas leaned back in his chair, looking at all of them with an air of approval.

'Oh, yes,' he said. 'I think we can manage that.'

19

Owain and his two companions stepped out of the ship into a quiet street in Pelidor. The shimmering doorway—which they had learned to call the teleport, though they were no closer to understanding how it worked—faded behind them. A light wind whispered along the paving stones. It was night, two days after they had first entered the ship.

Gildas was not with them. He had already been set down near the old mine workings, where they had met. He had a consignment of wood waiting there for him to collect.

'My excuse for being away,' he explained. 'I'll come through the gates in the normal way, first thing in the morning. If you need me, come to the carpenter's shop.'

The ship had dropped them down closer to the craftsmen's quarters than the Street of the Councillors, but they had most of the night in front of them, and no reason for haste. Their two days' rest on board the ship had strengthened them, and they knew now what they had to do. Silently, keeping to the shadows, they made their way to Severan's old house.

An hour later they stood outside it. As Hilarion took out the key, Owain looked up and saw above the door, faded and battered by neglect, but still discernible, the device of the falcon's head. If he had kept his eyes open, he reflected, when he first arrived in Pelidor, he might have solved the mystery several days earlier.

Hilarion unlocked the door and swung it open. Inside, everything was dark, but once they had closed the door behind them, and Hilarion was relocking it from the inside, Owain lit a lantern that Gildas had given him. They saw that they were standing in a wide hall with doors leading off it and a staircase at the far end. Richeldis looked around her.

'This hasn't been shut up for two years,' she said.

'No,' Hilarion explained. 'My father comes here sometimes. And servants from the citadel keep it clean.'

Richeldis nodded as if satisfied. 'Perhaps he comes to make sure the ring is still here.'

She crossed the hall to push open the nearest door. The room beyond was still furnished with a table and chairs, though the walls were bare of hangings.

'You stay here, Hilarion,' she directed. 'If you sit where you can see the door to the street, you can warn us if anyone comes. Owain and I will search.'

Hilarion nodded agreement, and Owain moved a chair to the right position for him, and used another to prop the door open.

'And before we start, Hilarion,' Richeldis went on, 'just tell me if there are any secret panels or hiding-places under the floor. We may as well get those out of the way first.'

'Nothing like that,' Hilarion said, smiling faintly.

'You don't know where Severan would be likely to hide something precious?'

He shook his head. 'His own room used to be the first one at the top of the stairs, but it might not be there.'

Richeldis sighed. 'So we have to search the whole house. Well, we've got the rest of the night. Come on, Owain, bring your lantern. We'll start upstairs and work down.'

Owain followed her up the stairs. They began to examine each room, but Owain soon began to feel that they would not find anything. There was quite a lot of furniture left in the house; almost every room had something in it, but everything was bare, and there were not many places where even something as small as a ring could be concealed. They poked the mattresses of the beds, and examined their covers for loose stitches. They looked underneath chairs, and around the openings of fireplaces.

There was a brief period of excitement when they discovered, in the last of the upstairs rooms, three chests in which hangings and cushions had been laid away. These had to be searched thoroughly, and the cushions prodded in case the ring was secreted inside, but the result was nothing.

Coming downstairs again, Owain examined the staircase itself. It was elaborately carved, with a ball on top of the newel post. Suddenly, an idea struck him. He began to try to unscrew the ball and caught his breath as it moved under his hand.

'What is it?' Richeldis asked.

'This is loose.'

He handed her the lantern so he could get both hands to it, and a moment later the heavy ball came away in his hands. Part of it was hollowed out, but to Owain's bitter disappointment, it was empty.

'Better put it back,' Richeldis said. 'It was a good idea.'

Hilarion was calling to them, wanting to know what they had discovered, and Richeldis went across to the room where he sat. Then she and Owain went on to search the downstairs rooms. This took longer, mostly because all the pots and pans had been left in the kitchen, and these had to be taken out and examined. It was hours later, and the first light of dawn was beginning to appear through chinks in the shutters, before they had finished and rejoined Hilarion. Owain realised that they had not searched the room in which he sat, but that was soon done.

Richeldis slumped into a chair beside the table, looking discouraged. 'I was so sure it was here!'

Owain sat beside her. 'It still could be. Behind a loose stone, or—Hilarion, is there a garden?'

'Just a small courtyard behind the house.'

'Then it could be there!' Owain said, getting to his feet.

Richeldis reached out to stop him. 'Not now, it's getting light. Besides, if it was in the courtyard, what would we do? Take up all the paving stones? Examine every stone in the wall? Dig it all up?' She rested her elbows on the table and her head on her hands. 'Somewhere we've made a mistake, but I can't see where.'

The light from the shuttered windows was growing stronger, and Owain thought he could hear sounds from the street outside. They had left it too late to leave the house safely; they would have to hide there until the following night. At least there were beds upstairs, if only bare mattresses, where they could sleep. He put out the lantern, and suggested going up to rest, but though Richeldis and Hilarion both nodded, no one made a move. It was as if that would have meant finally admitting defeat.

Richeldis had taken out her wooden ball, and was absent-mindedly playing with it, separating each of the nesting balls until she came to the centre. The smallest ball was of smooth, polished wood. Inside it, Petroc used to hide a surprise gift for the child—a tiny carved animal, or a silver penny, or a sweetmeat. Owain picked it up and tried to prise it apart.

'That one doesn't open,' Richeldis said.

'Oh yes it does. But something's sticking.'

Unwilling to be defeated, he took out his belt knife.

'Be careful!'

Richeldis sounded annoyed. Very delicately, Owain inserted the knife point into the almost invisible join between the two halves of the ball. Suddenly scarlet flowered under his hands. He jerked back, half believing it was his own blood, dropping the knife, the two halves of the ball, the tightly wadded scarlet silk that was springing out of its folds, and something else, something heavy—a ring that rolled across the table and winked gold and smouldering red in a shaft of sunlight.

Wordlessly they stared at it. And into the silence came the beat of footsteps, quick and decisive, approaching down the street and stopping outside the door. There was a pause, and then the sound of a key being inserted into the lock.

'Who has a key?' Owain whispered.

Hilarion had gone paper-white.

'Only—'

His voice died away as the door opened and the tall, dark figure of Severan was outlined in the doorway. He closed it and stood for a moment, smiling.

'Well! Someone told me that they heard movement in here, and saw a light, but I never thought that....'

Lightly, rapidly, he crossed the hall and stood on the threshold of the room, suddenly transfixed as his eyes fell on the ring. Hilarion struggled to his feet and snatched up the knife Owain had let fall. His father looked at him, something new in his face, something Owain could not define. His voice was shaking a little—with fear or laughter?—as he said, 'Don't be absurd, boy.'

Gently he took hold of Hilarion's wrist and removed the knife, which he tossed onto the table, scarcely glancing at it. Hilarion gave in without a struggle, and sank back into his chair with a stifled sob. And Severan stepped forward and took up the ring.

For a few seconds he turned it this way and that, letting the great ruby catch the light. 'Pretty,' he murmured. Then he moved round the table towards Richeldis, who rose to her feet, almost, but not quite, shrinking from him. Severan's smile suddenly became real, vivid. He reached forward, took her hand, and placed the ring upon it.

'There,' he said with a sigh. 'Now it's where it belongs.'

And he raised the hand that bore the ring, and kissed it.

20

Richeldis snatched her hand away and took a step back.

'Don't be ridiculous!' she snapped.

She might as well not have spoken.

'I have always wondered,' Severan remarked, 'why everyone automatically assumed that Lady Isolda's child was a boy.'

He glanced round at the three of them. By now their attention was riveted on him.

'Forgive me, you are guests in my house, though the circumstances are...unusual. Please be seated.

We have a great deal to talk about, and we may as well be comfortable.'

Owain groped for a chair and sat on it, and after a brief hesitation, Richeldis reluctantly did the same. She was about to take the ring off, but Severan covered her hand gently and prevented her.

'No, my dear. It's yours. Listen.'

Even then, he looked round at them again before he spoke. This time his eyes lingered on Hilarion. His son was rigid, his hands clenched on the arms of his chair so that the knuckles showed white. At last Severan gave him a little nod, as if passing him some kind of private message, took a deep breath, and began.

'Sixteen years ago, Pelidor was in confusion. The lands to the south—not ruled directly by Pelidor, but by two of the Lords Councillors— were fighting off an attack by bands of hillmen trying to extend their lands. Lord Cador led a company of men from Pelidor to help his allies in their war, and in that battle he was killed. Word came to Lady Isolda just a few days before she expected to give birth to her child.'

Richeldis shifted impatiently; Owain guessed that all this was familiar to her.

'Another man who was killed in the same battle was the husband of Lady Isolda's waiting woman, and she was also expecting a child. She gave birth to a boy, and died. Perhaps in her grief for her husband she did not wish to live. Lady Isolda's daughter was born on the following day.'

Owain was now beginning to make sense of

what he knew, but he would not have dreamed of interrupting.

'Lady Isolda knew that Arven would be Lord Regent, and she was afraid for the safety of her daughter. She also felt responsible for the little boy, who had no one now to take care of him. She knew she had to make Arven believe that she had hidden her own child—' He broke off suddenly, and the formal manner he had assumed to tell the story fell away from him.

'Richeldis, my dear, do you think that your mother would have sent you away to be brought up by strangers, however worthy or reliable? Especially when she had to train you for the task of ruling in Pelidor? It was the other child, the boy, that she sent away, and I found a suitable home for him.'

Owain bit back an interruption.

'I took him far enough away,' Severan continued, 'to a household where I thought he would be cared for. The servants who were in the secret I paid well, and suggested that they discreetly disappeared. Our tracks were covered very efficiently.'

For the first time, Richeldis seemed to recognise the truth of what she was being told.

'She was my mother?' she asked.

'She was.'

'But she told me—'

'She could not entrust a secret like that to a child who might have given it away. She always intended to tell you the truth when you came of age and could claim Pelidor for your own.'

'And then she died,' Richeldis said.

'Yes. Though in the last words she spoke, she told you the truth. She said, "My daughter...." She was always an intensely practical woman.'

The great ring flashed as Richeldis suddenly hid her face in her hands. Her voice came as if she was speaking through tears.

'I wish I'd known! I wish I could have told her....'

Severan reached forward and gently drew her hands away.

'She knew. You could have been no more to her if she had been able to own you as hers. You always were her daughter.'

With a great effort, Richeldis conquered her tears.

'And you knew...' she said.

Severan's slightly mocking smile returned.

'I knew,' he repeated. 'I discussed the whole fate of Pelidor with your mother when word came of Lord Cador's death. We knew what Arven would do—most importantly that he would banish the priests of the Lord and try to cut Fern off from trade and friendship with Centre. He had made his views clear enough when his brother was alive. Lady Isolda and I knew that his power would go unchallenged for sixteen years. We couldn't change that, but we decided that we could lessen the damage he could do. And so I turned traitor. I became Arven's man. As his steward, I had his confidence, he listened to my advice, and I was responsible for carrying out his orders. I've done a great deal that I regret, but I think I've prevented more harm by being where I was.'

Owain could see by the look Richeldis was giving him, that she was not sure whether she could believe Severan or not. Severan recognised it too.

'You don't trust me,' he said, sighing faintly. 'I have played my part too well, it seems. But—look.'

He undid the top fastening of his robe, drew out something on the end of a leather thong, and held it out towards Richeldis on the palm of his hand. It was a cross. Owain, with a stifled exclamation, recognised the cross that the pedlar had brought to Pelidor.

'Arven or Jerold would have thrown it on the fire,' Severan said. 'I thought it deserved a better fate. My dear, I am truly a friend of the Church, and your friend too, if you will have me.'

Richeldis was gazing intently at the cross.

'Then why didn't you tell me all this when I came to Pelidor?' she asked him.

'Two reasons. First, you were still not quite of age. Second, I had no idea where to find the ring, for that was the one thing Lady Isolda had not told me. I thought perhaps you knew, but when I questioned you, I was sure you were telling the truth, and that puzzled me. I played for time by convincing Arven that you would be more likely to co-operate if you were treated well. I decided that I would wait until your birthday—' he paused, half laughing—'as in fact I have done. For today, if I'm right, you come of age.'

'So I do!' Richeldis exclaimed. 'I'd forgotten.'

'It's fortunate that the ring has come to light at the same time.'

Richeldis bent her head, and really looked at the ring for the first time since Severan had put it on her finger.

'It was inside the ball...' she murmured. 'Lady Isolda really had given it to Pelidor's heir, though I didn't realise it.' In her turn she was overtaken by laughter. 'Do you know, I almost sold the ball, for five silver pieces!'

'As well you didn't, my dear,' Severan said, sharing her amusement. 'Though if you were in need of money, you could have come to me.'

'No I couldn't,' Richeldis retorted candidly, 'since I wanted it to bribe the guard to release that pedlar from Centre.'

Severan sighed.

'Ah, yes, that pedlar! A nuisance if ever there was one.'

'A nuisance?'

'For getting himself into trouble at that particular time. Oh, I was always well aware that there was a group of the servants of the Lord working in Pelidor—though I didn't feel safe enough to reveal myself to them. I managed to hide their existence from Arven, until that tedious young man, Jerold, forced it on his knowledge. By then, the time I had to work with had shrunk to a matter of days. I would have tried to postpone his questioning until you, Hilarion, took the problem out of my hands.'

He turned to face his son for the first time. Now he was deeply serious.

'Hilarion, the one real mistake I made in all this business has been to keep you ignorant. Only two people knew of my true loyalties—Lady Isolda and your mother, and she made me promise to tell you nothing. I agreed, because I was afraid for your safety. But there are worse things than danger, and one of them is the life I made you lead. Can you forgive me?'

Hilarion was silent, though his eyes never left his father's face. When Severan spoke again, there was a note of desperation in his voice.

'I saw you realise that your father was a traitor. I saw you clinging to your own faith and truth through it all. I admired you, but I could say nothing.'

The whole room was silent, except for the sound of Hilarion's ragged breathing.

'But you were there!' he said at last. 'By the river—hunting us down!'

'And where did you expect me to be?' Severan's anxiety dissolved in impatience. 'How could I have helped you by staying to wring my hands in the citadel? I trust you heard my hint to you to cross the river?'

'You knew we were there?' Owain could not repress the exclamation.

'Of course. You had left a distinct trace on the bank where you went in. Jerold failed to notice it, since I was standing on it. He is not, perhaps, the most subtle of adversaries.'

He moved round the table to stand in front of Hilarion.

'We were friends once,' he said, 'when you were too young to ask questions. Have I destroyed all that? Is it too late?'

Hilarion looked up at him, and then, unsteadily,

rose to his feet. Severan, putting out a hand to support him, was suddenly embracing him fiercely, while Hilarion clung to him and gave way to silent, desperate weeping.

Owain felt his own throat close with tears. Meeting Richeldis' eyes, he realised that she felt the same. He wished they could have left father and son together, but there was too much, following on the discoveries of the last hour, that had to be decided.

'What do we do now?' he said, half to himself.

His words drew Severan's attention. The brief storm was already passing; the steward was recovering, though not quite successfully, the mask of detached mockery which he presented to the world.

'What we do now is consider our next move. And before we do that, I should like to know a little more about you. You've been involved in all of this, but I still don't see how you fit in.'

'Me? Oh, I'm no one in particular.' Owain grinned out of a relief so vast that he was only just becoming aware of it. 'I'm Owain. I'm the son of Petroc the carpenter.'

21

Severan stared at him.

'I'm the baby you took to Petroc,' Owain explained.

He was enjoying himself now, finding it hard to suppress his laughter. He no longer had to bear the burden of rule in Pelidor. He knew the answer to the problem of who he was and where he belonged, and it was a very simple answer, after all.

'Owain!' Richeldis exclaimed. 'I thought all along it was you! Do you mind?'

'Mind?' His laughter broke through now. 'Richeldis, I couldn't have ruled in Pelidor. I wouldn't have known where to start.'

'But you know, Lady,' Severan said, and there was something in his tone which sobered Owain rapidly. 'You have good sense, warmth and the courage. And you will need them all in the days to come.'

Richeldis sat looking at him thoughtfully.

'It isn't going to be easy, is it?'

'No, it is not. So we must decide our next move.'

Infinitely careful, he let Hilarion sink back into his seat again, though he kept a hand lightly on his shoulder. Hilarion could not tear his eyes away from his father's face.

'Today is the meeting of the Lords Councillors,' Severan began.

'Do you think I should present myself to them?'

'Yes, Lady, I do.'

'But Arven might kill her!' Owain protested.

Severan gave him a long, cool look.

'That is the risk she takes,' he said.

'But—' Owain began to protest again, and then choked the words back. It was no use trying to protect Richeldis. She had to go out into danger, now and in the future, with no thought for her own safety, beyond what was best for her people. With a sudden pang, he felt that he was losing her as a friend.

'If I go before the Lords,' she was continuing, 'what do you think they will do?'

'I can tell them the story, and you have the ring....' Severan's voice died and then gathered confidence. 'I think they will accept you.'

'And Arven?'

Severan considered for a moment before he answered that.

'I've lived close to him for sixteen years,' he replied. 'He's not a cruel man. He has no love of killing—'

'He would have killed her when she was a baby!' Owain could not repress the interruption.

'I think not. It's possible, but...no, my dear, if Arven had known who you were, I don't think he would have killed you. He would have brought you to the court, taken care of you, showered you with wealth—and made quite sure you would never grow up to be the sort of person who could take over Pelidor. You would never have known the true God. Also, as you're a girl, in the fullness of time he would have married you to Jerold.'

Richeldis shuddered. 'Over my dead body.'

'That might have been your alternative,' replied Severan. 'However, as it is, if the Lords Councillors accept you, he has nothing to gain from your death. They would never take him for their Lord again. He has nothing more to play for.'

Silence fell as he finished speaking. Richeldis was deep in thought, and no one dared to interrupt. It was not long before she asked, 'When does the meeting begin?'

'When I left the citadel, the Lords were already assembling. They will be in Council now.'

Richeldis stood up and shook out her skirts. 'Then what are we waiting for?'

When Owain stepped out into the street once more, blinking against the sunlight, he realised that the morning was half over. The talk with Severan had taken longer than he had realised. He looked up the street; at the top, not far away, was the gate of the citadel with its guards on each side.

'Aren't they still looking for us?' he asked.

'Of course,' Severan replied. 'And I have found you. You're my prisoners, so look suitably dejected, please.'

Owain supposed that he looked frightened enough, when he thought what lay ahead for Richeldis. He fell in at her side as they moved slowly up the street, followed by Severan and Hilarion.

'I understand now,' Richeldis said, 'why my Lady gave you to Severan, and why she didn't worry about what had happened to you. She knew Severan was faithful, if no one else did.'

Owain nodded, but he was surprised that

Richeldis could make conversation at a time like this. 'Aren't you afraid?' he asked.

She tossed back her hair; her face was serious, but her eyes sparkled.

'Yes—oh, but Owain, it isn't a bad fear. It's knowing—knowing I have to do it, and no one else can. And I think it will be all right.'

'I hope it will,' Owain responded.

Already they were approaching the gates. As they passed through, there was a stir among the guards which Severan quelled. He snapped his fingers at a couple of them, who fell in behind. They went on towards the Hall of Council.

It looked very different from the day when the prisoner's escape had been discovered. Then it had been crowded; today it was empty except for the Lords Councillors. Ten chairs were placed before the dais in a semi-circle, their backs to the door. Nine of them were occupied; the tenth, Owain realised, must be Severan's. On the dais, Arven was standing, and on another seat towards the back of the dais was Jerold, present, but not a member of the Council. Arven was speaking.

'...security of Pelidor, and in fact the security of all Fern,' were the first words Owain could distinguish as he and his companions approached the doors. 'The question of the succession is one we should settle as soon as possible. I'm not getting any younger, and I, and you and all our people have the right to know what will happen after my time. My Lords, the heir of Pelidor is lost. And even if, in the future, he were found, what good would he be to Pelidor? He knows nothing of the problems we face. He has never been trained to rule. Whereas I, my Lords, have a son to follow me—Jerold here. You all know him.'

Owain reflected that knowing Jerold would hardly persuade anyone to accept him as a future Lord of Pelidor. But perhaps it looked different if you happened to be his father. He lost the next few words of Arven's speech, and when he started listening again, the Lord Regent had moved on.

'...asking you to make the only possible decision, in confirming me as—'

'With your leave, my Lord,' Severan interposed smoothly, 'it is not the only possible decision.'

He moved forward quickly, shepherding Richeldis and ignoring Arven's exclamation when he realised the presence of the fugitives. He turned his back on Arven, and faced the Lords Councillors in their semi-circle of chairs. Owain noticed that he was still openly wearing the cross.

'My Lords, I present to you the heir of Pelidor, Lady Richeldis, the daughter of Cador and Isolda. She comes of age today, she wears the ring of Pelidor, and she is here to claim her inheritance.'

His voice soared over the clamour that broke out before he had finished speaking. Two or three of the Lords had sprung to their feet. Arven stood motionless, silent, but Jerold was beside him, grabbing at his arm and shouting something that was lost in the general noise. Owain and Hilarion edged closer, but Richeldis, outwardly unmoved, waited quietly for the tumult to die down. When it did, it was to Arven that she spoke.

'My Lord, I knew nothing of my birth until this morning. My Lord Severan—'

'Severan!' Arven interrupted. There was gathering anger in his face, but it was directed at the steward, not Richeldis. 'What lies are these you're telling us?'

'No lies, my Lord.'

Clearly, as if he had prepared his speech—and perhaps he had—Severan repeated the story he had already told, for the benefit of Arven and the Lords Councillors. They were silent now, weighing his every word. When he had finished, Arven said, 'What are you asking, Severan—for the Council to accept this chit of a girl as ruler of Pelidor?'

'This chit of a girl is Pelidor's rightful heir.'

Owain watched Arven intently, and wished he could see the faces of the other Lords. They were murmuring among themselves, and there had been no protest, no suggestion, even from Arven, that Severan's story was not the truth.

'My Lord Arven,' Richeldis said, 'I don't want you as my enemy. I think you're wrong in what you want for Pelidor and for Fern, but I value your experience, and if you would accept a place on the Council, I—'

'No!'

The roar of outrage came not from Arven, but from Jerold.

'It's all lies!' he shouted. 'It's all a plot of that....' He gestured wildly towards Severan. 'Don't listen to him!'

His father turned to him, beginning to speak, but his words were cut off as Jerold leaped from the dais. A knife flashed in his upraised hand. Severan, caught unawares, could not reach him, and it was Hilarion who flung himself forward, thrusting his staff between Jerold and Richeldis, while Owain grabbed at the hand that held the knife. They fell and scuffled on the ground together. Owain's eyes were on the deadly knife that still waved wildly somewhere above his head. He could hear shouting—the Lords, and Arven's voice above them all, but could not make out the words.

Then, all at once, there was silence. Owain thrust himself onto his knees. Beside him, Arven and Severan held Jerold, his arms pinioned beside him. The knife lay on the floor at their feet. Owain reached for it, and saw the smear of blood on the blade before he realised that on his other side lay Hilarion, unmoving.

Leaving Jerold to his father, Severan knelt at Hilarion's side. Richeldis whispered, 'No.' Then, at the touch of his father's hand, Hilarion stirred and struggled to sit up, clutching at his left arm. The sleeve of his robe was slashed, and blood oozed between his fingers. He looked very white, and glad to lean back against his father's shoulder.

'My Lady.' It was Arven who spoke, and Richeldis turned to him, startled to be addressed like that, especially from her enemy. 'My Lady, I ask your forgiveness. I should have schooled this boy better than that he should draw a weapon in the Hall of Council. He has no right to rule here if he cannot rule himself. I admit your claim on Pelidor, and I leave it to you. Your ways are not my ways.'

There was no defeat in the way he spoke; Owain had known him for a proud man, but at last he realised that his pride was drawn from trying to do right as he saw it. Severan had understood him. Roughly Arven thrust Jerold forward, through the half-circle of the waiting Lords, and out through the doors at the bottom of the hall. Richeldis stared after him as the sound of his footsteps died away.

22

Three days had passed since the meeting of the Lords Councillors. Richeldis had adjourned it as soon as Arven had departed, to let Hilarion be cared for, and to give the Lords a chance to catch up with events that had moved too quickly for most of them. They had made no official decision as to whether they would accept Richeldis as Lady of Pelidor.

For all that, Owain reflected, there did not seem to be much doubt about it. Richeldis was spending her time in earnest discussion with Severan and the Lords; one long evening she spent with Arven. Owain felt a little lonely and a little out of place, so he took to visiting Hilarion who was confined to his bed and fiercely impatient at being forced to rest. The wound Jerold had given him was not serious, but the strain of his days as a fugitive had caught up with him, and he was forced, at last, to give in to bodily weakness.

On the third day, however, Owain arrived to find Hilarion up and dressed. He seemed in high spirits.

'Haven't you heard?' he asked. 'There's to be another meeting, and we're invited to be present. My father has just been to tell me.'

There was a happy pride about the way he said 'my father', and Owain reflected that whatever happened at the meeting, that breach at least had been healed. Hilarion was wearing the falcon ring again. It had meant nothing to him while he believed his father was a traitor, but Owain could see that now he treasured it.

As they left the room, Owain noticed that Hilarion was using a handsome staff of polished wood, bound with silver. He looked twice at it before he realised that it was the same ash sapling he had cut in the forest. Remembering that day suddenly made it easy for Owain to decide what he was going to do next; really, he had known it ever since he discovered he was not the heir of Pelidor.

Waiting for them outside the Hall of Council was Richeldis herself.

'So there you are!' she exclaimed, with a trace of her old, mischievous smile. 'I've been waiting for you, to start the meeting.'

'What's going to happen?' Owain asked, still rather nervous.

'Nothing to worry about. The Lords have decided to accept me.'

'And what about Arven?'

'Arven still stands by what he said. You know, I think Jerold did me a favour by trying to kill me. It shocked his father; I think it showed him what his policies have led to.'

'And where is Jerold now?' Hilarion asked.

Richeldis gave him a look of catlike satisfaction.

'Banished from court. Not by me; his father sent him to his own estates in the north. And there, as far as I'm concerned, he can stay indefinitely.'

She turned and put her hand on the door handle, ready to enter the hall, and then quickly turned back. For a moment her air of brisk efficiency wavered.

'I'm sorry about Arven. I'd like him on the Council, if—'

'After all he's done to you!' Owain interrupted indignantly.

'He's done very little to me,' Richeldis said. 'And no one has ever called him an evil man. But he followed the wrong road—a road that might have led him to kill or torture his enemies, and to hunt down anyone he thought would threaten his power.' She hesitated, and went on more thoughtfully, 'I've talked to him, you know, since we came back. He can see now that it was the wrong road, and he's like a man wandering without any direction. I wonder if he'll ever find the right path.'

'You can show him,' Owain said, wondering even as he spoke whether Arven could ever learn the humility he would need to work with Richeldis as his Lady.

'I can show him, yes,' she replied. 'I've tried to. But only Arven can make the decision.'

Then she smiled, and straightened up, as if she was forcing herself to be cheerful.

'We must begin the meeting. Come in. You can sit at the back of the dais. You'll find one friend of yours waiting for us.'

She opened the door and led the way. Wondering what she meant, Owain followed.

The Lords Councillors were already assembled in their semi-circle of chairs. They rose to their feet as Richeldis entered and took her seat on the dais. As he moved to his own seat, Owain understood what Richeldis meant—for already there was Gildas, the priest-carpenter. He smiled at Owain and Hilarion, but could say nothing as Richeldis was already opening the meeting.

When she had welcomed the Lords, one of their number got up and made a rambling speech, the gist of which was that the Lords Councillors acknowledged Richeldis as the daughter of Cador and Isolda, and accepted her as Lady of Pelidor. Though it was the culmination of what they had hoped for, Owain found the man impossible to listen to. Instead he looked around the hall, and noticed one or two changes.

Three days ago, there had been ten chairs ranged before the dais, nine for the Lords Councillors, and the tenth for Severan. Now there were twelve, and two remained empty. Owain wondered who was meant to occupy those two chairs.

Severan was already there, making notes of the speech on a lap desk, with a faintly ironic expression that made Owain wonder what he felt about the long-winded Lord's style of delivery.

At last the speech was over, and Richeldis rose again, briefly thanked the Lord, and then paused, collecting all the audience with her eyes.

'My Lords,' she began, 'I stand at the beginning of my rule in Pelidor, and for the time being I want as little change as possible. Don't be afraid that I'll interfere with how you choose to rule your own lands.

'However, some change there must be. My father, Lord Cador, welcomed the ships from Centre, and he believed that Fern should be proud of its place as one of the Six Worlds. From now on, the Lords of Centre will once more send their ships to Pelidor.

'My father also believed that we should trust in the God who made all worlds, and that we should try to live the life he laid down for us. I hereby revoke the banishment of the priests of God, and I promise the favour of Pelidor to all who follow his way, especially those who stayed faithful through all the dangerous years.'

She turned, and with a smile and a gesture brought Gildas to his feet.

'Gildas, you have done God's work in Pelidor, and now I ask you to go on doing it, to gather and encourage the Lord's people with all the help that I can give you. And so that you have the power you need to do what needs to be done, I offer you a seat on the Council.'

There was a stir of surprise among the Lords when they heard this, but Gildas had obviously been expecting it. He bowed to Richeldis, and calmly came down from the dais and took his place in the eleventh seat.

'We shall speak more of this later,' Richeldis said, and then turned directly to Severan. 'My Lord Steward.'

Severan rose and inclined his head.

'My Lord, you served admirably in your double role, balancing your friendship with Isolda against your service to Arven.'

The tone she used did not make her words sound like praise. At Owain's side, Hilarion was looking rather troubled; he, at least, did not know what was coming next. Severan waited quietly, raising his brows a fraction, but otherwise remaining impassive.

'In considering your sixteen years in Arven's service,' Richeldis went on, 'it is my decision that you should be stripped of your rank of steward, for I will not have you serve me as you served him.'

Still impassive, but without taking his eyes off her face, Severan unfastened his silver chain, stepped forward to lay it on the dais at Richeldis' feet, and then stepped back and waited. Glancing at Hilarion, Owain saw him suddenly whiten, and reached out a hand to him, almost afraid that he would interrupt.

Richeldis looked down at the chain and then back at Severan.

'That was necessary, my Lord, because I have another task for you. You shall be Lord Warden of

Pelidor, and everything in the city shall be under your control, and as such, you shall be a full member of the Council. And you shall train your son to be Lord Warden after you.'

Severan bowed and took his seat again with a glimmer of a smile.

Owain was certain that, whatever had been discussed in private, the steward had not expected that. He himself let out a long sigh of relief; he could feel Hilarion shaking. Stealing a glance at his friend, he saw tears in his eyes, but he also began to understand what Hilarion might be like when he was really happy.

'And your first task, my Lord,' Richeldis was continuing, 'will be to find me another competent steward.'

She looked round the assembled Lords once again.

'And now the Council is complete,' she said, 'except for one. The twelfth place is for my Lord Arven, if he should choose to come and claim it.'

On the last words, she suddenly sounded less sure of herself. Owain understood how much it meant to her that Arven should give her his support. Without it, there would be a flaw in her coming to power in Pelidor, and the shadow of Arven, a self-imposed exile on his own estates, would always be over her. And the twelfth place still remained empty.

As Owain watched her, Richeldis shook her head slightly, as if she was banishing the problem of Arven. Then she turned to him.

'I have one more task before I close this meeting, my Lords,' she said. 'And that is a pleasant one. I present to you Owain, son of Petroc the carpenter.'

She beckoned Owain to the front of the dais, and, feeling extremely awkward, he got up and went to her.

'Owain, but for your friendship, I should not be standing here, and the ring of Pelidor would never have been discovered. What can I give you as a reward?'

Owain stopped feeling awkward, because he knew the answer to that. He spoke to her as if they were alone together, without the audience of assembled Lords; friends as they had always been and as they always would be.

'I don't want anything, except perhaps a little money and an escort on the road. I'm going home.'

'Back to Petroc?'

'Back to my parents. I've still got a trade to learn.'

Richeldis smiled and took his hands.

'But you'll come back? You're still my friend, Owain. And the court can always use a master carpenter.'

He was about to reply, when there was a movement at the other end of the hall. The double doors swung open. Owain felt Richeldis' hands tighten on his, and saw the glad relief in her eyes before he realised the cause of it. It was Arven. Silently, gazing straight ahead of him, he stalked down the length of the hall. There was a murmur among the other Lords, which he ignored. Releasing Owain, Richeldis drew herself up, and managed to say, 'Welcome, my Lord.'

149

Arven made no response except a curt nod of the head as he halted. Then, as the muttered comments died into silence, he took the seat that was waiting for him, twelfth and last of the Lords Councillors in the Hall of Pelidor.

* * *

Owain, mounted on a solid little chestnut pony, reined in at the side of the road, and raised a hand in farewell as Lord Kynan's followers filed past him. Kynan, Owain's own Lord, had been present at the meetings of the Lords Councillors, and Owain had travelled home among his retinue. Now, at last, their paths were dividing; Owain looked down on the rooftops of the town he had left so many weeks before.

It was evening. Behind him, red streaks still showed in the western sky. Ahead, a few stars were glimmering, and in the town lights were springing up from lamps and hearth fires. As the last of Kynan's men disappeared into the gathering dusk, Owain turned his pony's head and urged it gently down the winding road into the valley.

The pony was a gift from Richeldis, the only one he had accepted of all she had offered him, apart from a small amount of money so that on the journey home he would not be quite dependent on Kynan. And he bore two other gifts. The silver clasp of his cloak, shaped like a pair of falcon's wings, had belonged to Hilarion. Severan had given him the cross that the pedlar had brought to Pelidor. But what meant more to him even than

these were gifts that could not be seen: their friendship, and his own certainty of who he was.

The soft earth of the road gave way to cobbles,
and his pony's steps sounded clearly in the evening
stillness. Owain was impatient now, his breath
coming faster. And at last he drew to a halt in the
familiar street, slid from the saddle, and pushed
open the door to Petroc's workshop.

The lamps were lit. His father was clearing up
from the day's work, sweeping shavings into a tidy
heap. As the door opened, he looked up, startled,
and then his slow, pleased smile spread across his
face. Before he could speak, Sarai came down the
passage from the house, a question dying on her
lips and her face alight.

'I'm home,' Owain said. 'Is supper ready?'

The Book And The Phoenix

by Cherith Baldry

Times are hard for most of the Six Worlds. Earth is long forgotten, left behind in a past age when technology brought men and women to the stars.

The old tales tell how, generations ago, the colonists brought with them a belief, a faith, a way of life. But that's almost forgotten now, just a dream for old men.

Until now. Young Cradoc will see a vision of the legendary phoenix that will lead him to a Book. It is only when he discovers the power in the Book that he also learns there are many who will want to destroy it—and anyone who attempts to protect it.

Phoenix

Published by Kingsway

Hostage Of The Sea

by Cherith Baldry

They came from over the sea, a nation of warriors intent on spreading their empire. When they descended upon a small kingdom that served the God of peace, the battle was short. And Aurion, the peaceful King's son, was the ideal hostage to secure victory.

Coming to the fearsome land of Tar-Askar, Aurion meets the strong and proud son of the warrior king. A most unlikely friendship develops—a bond of love that will prove a greater threat to the Tar-Askan empire than the weapons of war.

Also by **CHERITH BALDRY** in the *Stories of the Six Worlds: The Book and the Phoenix.*

 *Phoenix*
Published by Kingsway

The Will Of Dargan

by Phil Allcock

Trouble has darkened the skies of the Realm: the Golden Sceptre crafted by the hands of Elsinoth the Mighty has been stolen. Courageous twins, Kess and Linnil, team up with an assorted company of elves and crafters—and set out to find it.

Their journey takes them through rugged mountains, gentle valleys and wild woods to the grim stronghold of Dargan the Bitter. Will they win back the Sceptre? The answer depends on their courage, friendship and trust.

Phoenix

Published by Kingsway

Oodles Of Poodles

by Andrew Wooding

When *Dickie Dustbin* met a genie in a coke can, he knew that life was going to change. *But not this much…*

Enter one *Charlie Digestives,* world-renowned poodle detective, in search of the dreaded *Clothes Line Snatcher*, who has even more wicked designs on the universe than whipping socks off clothes lines. Will *Charlie* catch up with the fiend before it's *too late for all life?* Will the real *Dickie* triumph over the vile life-size photocopy of himself *and* discover what true love is all about?

Phoenix

Published by Kingsway

The Muselings

by Ed Wicke

One day three scruffy children from an orphanage in the country have a surprise. Rachel, Robert and Alice fall *up* a tree into another world!

Why have they been brought into the land that scheming Queen Jess calls her own? The Queen and the children would *both* like to know, and as they try to find out, they stumble into hilarious and hair-raising adventures. Here we meet Lord Lrans, mad on hunting; the Reverend Elias, beloved but misunderstood vicar; Ballbody, a round, bouncy fellow…and the Muselings—kind, furry creatures whose world the children have fallen into.

Then Elias faces Queen Jess on a hilltop, and everything changes.

Phoenix

Published by Kingsway

The Curse Of Craigiburn

by Jennifer Rees Larcombe

They said that Craigiburn was cursed. The curtains were always drawn, and it was a sad family that lived in it.

James Brodie lived there now, with his father. What was the curse? Why would no one tell him? And why did the Ugly Man of the Forest send him away when he found out who he was?

Jamie was determined to find the answer to his questions. Little did he know how events would conspire to help him, especially once an old book came back from the distant past.

Phoenix

Published by Kingsway

Hagbane's Doom

A tale of heroism, adventure, and the age-old conflict between good and evil

by John Houghton

Introducing...

Peter, Sarah and Andrew—three ordinary children caught up in an adventure that proves to be far from ordinary.

Trotter, Aldred, Stiggle and company—a band of lovable animals united in the fight against a wicked tyrant.

Hagbane—an evil witch who rules the Great Forest with a bitter hatred and an iron will.

Oswain—a prince whose destiny not even he will fully understand until he looks into the enchanted pool.

Children of all ages (and there's no upper limit!) will enjoy this gripping fantasy which portrays the power of love and goodness in the face of evil.

Phoenix

Published by Kingsway

Tracy And The Warriors

by Lynda Neilands

Tracy is a nine-year-old Brownie, and she is homesick. Sent to stay with her grim aunt and her wild cousin, she pours out all her woes in letters to God.

Her cousin and his friends (a gang of so-called warriors) lose no time in making life difficult for Tracy, but she finds help from the visiting Circus. When the warriors burn down Carlo the clown's caravan, all seems lost. Is it possible for anything good to come out of such a disaster?

LYNDA NEILANDS is the writer of *The Brownie Handbook*. She lives with her family in Dublin, in the Republic of Ireland.

Phoenix
Published by Kingsway